venue

an international literary magazine

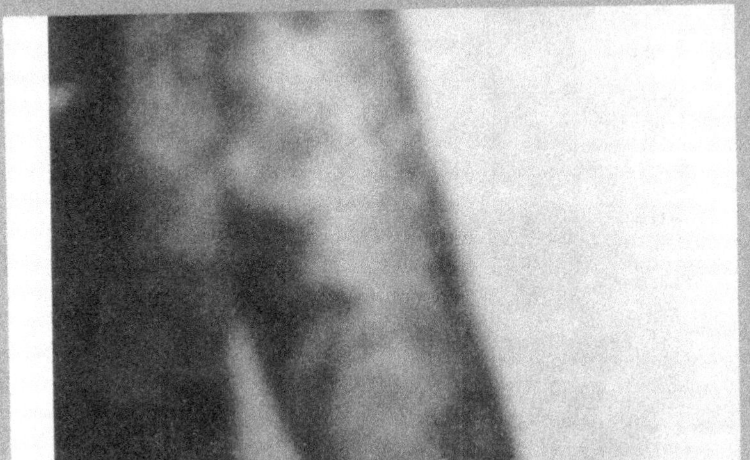

the
killers

2

1998

©1998 OPA (Overseas Publishers Association) Amsterdam B. V. Published under license under the G+B Arts International imprint, a part of The Gordon and Breach Publishing Group.

Rights revert to the authors upon publication.

Venue is published four times a year (December, March, June, September).
ISBN 90-5701-381-9
ISSN 1027-0272

Subscriptions and inquiries should be addressed to **International Publishers Distributor** in care of one of the addresses below:

P.O. Box 32160
Newark, NJ 07102 USA
Telephone: 1-800-545-8398
Fax: 973-643-7676

IPD Marketing Services
P.O. Box 310
Queen's House, Don Road
St. Helier, Jersey
Channel Islands JE4 OTH
Telephone: 44(0)118-956-0080
Fax: 44(0)118-956-8211

Kent Ridge, PO Box 1180
Singapore 911106
Republic of Singapore
Telephone: 65 741-6933
Fax: 65 741-6922

Yohan Western Publications
  Distribution Agency
3-14-9, Okubo,
Shinjuku-ku
Tokyo 169, Japan
Telephone: 81 3 3208-0186
Fax: 81 3 3208 5308

Subscription rate:
One year (four issues):
  US $38.00
  GB £26.00
  ECU 32.00

Trade Distribution:
Distributed Art Publishers
155 Sixth Avenue, 2nd Floor
New York, NY 10013-1507
Telephone: 212-627-1999
Fax: 212-627-9484

Unsolicited manuscripts — FICTION and ESSAYS — are welcomed. Manuscripts should be typed and double spaced and will not be returned unless accompanied by a stamped, self-addressed envelope. Submission will be taken to imply that the manuscript has never been published previously in any form and has not been simultaneously offered to any other publication. We do not accept unsolicited submissions for the FORUM.

DESIGN BY: *Terry Berkowitz*

Contents

PHOTOGRAPHS *Joanne Ross*

THE KILLERS

The Baker's Ongoing Resurrection

Ida Fink

FOR WEEKS NOW THEY'VE BEEN BRINGING the baker Weiskranz back to life, only to kill him again, always in the same ingenious way. They start off with a brief topographical description, just to give the lay of the land, and proceed with their version of the baker's last moments. The accuracy of the account depends on the memory of each teller.

Among those, for example, who mention the flat cement structure at the back of the camp, there are some who refer to it as a "pool." This implies that the structure was not built for the sole purpose of drowning prisoners who were so weak that when they were tossed inside and made to lie in the shallow water they simply drowned. Others, however, maintain that this "pool" was designed expressly for that purpose. Still others have no idea of its existence.

It's the same with the shed. Many assume it was used to store shovels, wheelbarrows and pickaxes, but there are those who are quick to add that it also served to store the bodies of people who had been murdered. For others the tool room is shrouded in the fog of forgetfulness.

And it's the same with Weiskranz, with one difference: everybody knows how he was murdered, and many saw it with their own eyes.

Day after day new details keep filling in the first rough sketch, but in the end certain parts remain completely blank: In which direction did the barrel roll with the baker inside it? Down the length of the square or across it? Did it stop when it ran into the wire fence, or did the prisoners stop it when the commandant ordered them to?

Of course these are not the only blank frames in this painstakingly assembled montage about dying in a barrel. There are more such imprecisions, which is why, during a bright hot summer many, many years after the tragic but at that time commonplace event, baker Weiskranz is forced to rise from the dead and die again, day after day.

ND BOTH RESURRECTION AND DEATH occur in slow motion; the camera notes every detail, even the most banal — it was about to rain; the farmers were raking hay — and every phase of the event itself.

It's five in the morning. The month of September. To find the exact date we would have to consult the Jewish calendar, since we're speaking about a Jewish holiday.

Barracks number 2. There are only ten barracks; the camp isn't very big.

It's five in the morning, and in the camp a new day is dawning.

No sooner has the day dawned than the accounts begin to diverge.

Some narrators claim that on that day Weiskranz did not get

up from his cot himself but was awoken by Kapo Heinz, who was inspecting the barracks and discovered the sick baker on top of his straw mattress and a bottle underneath. And that Heinz immediately reported the offense to the commandant. As far as the bottle is concerned, everyone agrees that it existed: Weiskranz had an infected bladder; he didn't have the strength to get up during the night. The discrepancies have to do with the timing. Did Kapo Heinz discover it on the same day that Weiskranz was murdered? That is, was the barrel a direct result of the bottle?

There are many who say: Yes. Absolutely. I remember exactly.

But there are also many who say that the incident with the bottle happened a week earlier, that the barrel had nothing to do with the bottle discovered by Heinz, that the barrel happened later.

Some say: It was five in the morning. At five we would get up to be counted. Kapo Heinz burst into the barracks, calling out *Aufstehen Kinder*! — wake up children, time for breakfast! — so everyone knew that Kapo Heinz had gotten up on the wrong side of bed. And everyone tried to sneak out of the barracks as quickly as possible, but not everyone succeeded, since Heinz was standing at the entrance doling out his "breakfast" with his stick, hitting this one on the head, and that one....

Afterward he inspected the barracks, which he didn't always do, and that's when he discovered the old baker Weiskranz, wrapped up in a blanket, lying on a lower bunk in the corner. He had been sick for several days. Benio, the barracks elder, hadn't reported Weiskranz, since Benio wasn't a bad guy and did what he could. But there wasn't much he could do. So Kapo Heinz was standing over Weiskranz, and old Weiskranz, already a Muselmann, was fast asleep.

Well, we said to ourselves, now you see him; now you don't. Today there's Weiskranz, but once Heinz hits him with his stick that will be that. However, the first thing Kapo Heinz did was bend over and take the bottle out from underneath the bunk. Weiskranz didn't have the strength to get up during the night and go to the bucket. It was only then that the kapo started yelling. He forgot all about using the stick and ran off to tell the commandant.

Kapo Heinz was — as everyone knows — the dog in charge of all the other dogs. The barracks elder, Benio, said to the baker: Weiskranz, you better get up and go to the boilers, because I can't cover for you anymore. So Weiskranz pulled himself off his bunk and marched off to sift coal at the *Kohlensieberei*, where the commandant showed up at ten o'clock along with the head kapo. They dragged him to the square and ordered him to crawl inside the barrel.

STILL OTHERS SAY: He was an elderly man, very pious. He worked in the *Kohlensieberei*, and within a month he had already turned into a Muselmann, since it was very hard labor. Benio, the barracks elder, covered for him, because Benio had a very pious father whom they had gassed in the main camp. Benio often said that Weiskranz reminded him of his father. That was the only reason he protected him, because usually Benio wasn't so nice. And then, when Kapo Heinz found the bottle underneath the baker's bed, Benio had a talk with Heinz, and the kapo didn't report it to the commandant. Weiskranz, weak and sick as he was, got up and went to the *Kohlensieberei* in order to avoid the infirmary — because if he wound up in the infirmary they would take him to the main camp, to the ovens. It wasn't until a week later that they killed him on the square, in the barrel. For a completely different reason....

Every morning, and these summer days are brighter and hotter than that day in September, the baker lies dozing on his bunk. Every day Kapo Heinz enters barracks number 2 and says the same thing about breakfast. Day after day he inspects the barracks, day after day the sick baker pulls himself from his bed and, supported by the other prisoners, stands on the square to be counted....

For a completely different reason, they say, and not until a week later. Benio was able to buy him out of the bottle business. But a week later the feeble, sick baker Weiskranz pulled himself from his bunk in the morning, went around the barracks and told the prisoners it was a day of fasting. He didn't line up for coffee in the morning. He was very pious and God-fearing; he fasted and wanted the others to fast as well. But no one fasted, only him. He could barely stand up on his feet and the commandant noticed that at once. Then Kapo Heinz told the commandant that the prisoner was weak because he was fasting, and the commandant looked around the square and pointed to the empty lime barrel.

"*In das Fass hinein!*" — "Into the barrel!" — he shouted. The head kapo stuffed Weiskranz into the barrel and ordered it to be rolled around the square, which dropped off toward the wire fence, beyond which flowed the river.

Others say: The commandant himself put him in the barrel and ordered the barrel to be rolled from the watchtower across the square.

Some say: They rolled the barrel for five minutes.

Some say: Ten minutes.

The commandant shouted: "*Genug!*"

The head kapo shouted: "*Genug!*"

All agree: When the barrel stopped rolling Weiskranz was no longer alive.

All agree: Everything happened between ten and eleven in the morning.

All agree: It was about to rain. In the field beyond the wire fence the farmers were raking hay.

For weeks now they've been bringing baker Weiskranz back to

life, only to kill him again, always in the same ingenious way. Every morning, Kapo Heinz bursts into barracks number 2; every morning the baker pulls himself from his bunk. Every morning, a thousand kilometers away, the commandant climbs down from the second floor of his three-bedroom house and raises the blinds of the shop in which he sells smoked meat; the head kapo sits down at his desk at the automobile company.

Neither of them has ever heard of baker Weiskranz, who for many more months, and maybe even years, will keep rising from the dead and dying in the barrel.

Translated by Philip Boehm and Francine Prose

Han Ong

MY HEAD SWAM THROUGH SO MANY STATES. But none of these states had yet been set on by science, and therefore they represented neither plus nor minus signs, nothing by which I could measure the progress of my days.

People shouted my name — my father's name, which rang in my ears like laughter or the slap of water on someone's surprised face — early in the morning to wake me, for no other reason than that they were professional motherfuckers paid to motherfuck. We were left to languish in our cells till nearly lunchtime but they wanted us awake for hours before that so we could reflect on the crimes that had gotten us here.

Instead, I let my mind go blank, cleansing myself of whatever was retained from last night's dreams, all the sick, sad, caramelized movie-hopes of my youth refusing to heed the eviction notice that my actions represented; they would creep out during the darkness of sleep when I was powerless to interfere, and would do dances inside my skull with the glee of subversives, Hope twisting away with Faith, Handsomeness curtseying in front of Grace, Ambition clutching himself in a slow solo to everyone's envy. Much as I tried to kill them, these things would not die.

I knew myself for three years by the things I did not, and would not, do. Deign to do. Just before the pitch-black of sleep, like a jump off some cliff, I would repeat that phrase over and over to myself.

I did not share my space with anyone.

I did not watch TV. Its sounds reached me from the rec room where the others congealed to witness the things they could not now have but which awaited them upon their return to normal lives, but I was unmoved.

I did not leave traces of myself, puddles of sweat, on the work-out equipment at the gym. I pumped and at the same time willed my pores dry, doing something harmful and irreversible to my body, I'm sure.

I felt superior to everything around me, and though this gave the air around my head a palpable stench of upper-classness, I went strangely untouched and unabused.

I read, that was how time marked itself, with the slow, crisp sound of pages turning one onto another, and what I read got me thinking. And most days what I thought about, or rather pictured in my head, was the world with a straight line — yellow like a road divider — drawn down its middle. On one side of this line stood people with outstretched fingers beginning an invisible clothesline which ended at us, who stood voiceless and with heads cast down on the other side. While we wore the grey uniforms of our situations, the people on the other side made a point of dressing like Crayola sticks. Each color seemed like an insult hurled at us.

I spent hours staring, too, at the grey bricks that walled me in. Each one had a distinct personality, some way of bouncing or absorbing light that made it revelatory, such that on certain days I was overwhelmed by the sheer number of those who wanted to destroy me: not just *one* wall but eighteen thousand bricks. Some had an indentation on their lower half that looked like small lips, and to these I would confess my sorrows and plead for forgiveness. I said to them, when they remained insensate like frigid socialite matrons, I said: Fuck you. Which was exactly what they echoed back to me.

M Y MOTHER CAME TO VISIT. Forgiveness could not have shaped itself into a more disgusting form. I sweated up and down seeing her make her entrance. Each of her footsteps was accompanied by a drumroll. She walked towards where I sat waiting for her to pick up the phone on her side. Meanwhile all I could do was smile the smile of the defeated. This was exactly the hole she'd forecast for me years before, and now that I was finally here she could not have been happier.

But I had my post-jail life staked out: Hightail out of her sight with the money she promised for the continued good behavior that would guarantee me an early release. But for now I did everything according to the dictates of a little voice in the back of my mind that I nicknamed Mr Mastermind. In my imagination this voice had a moustache and two hands that he constantly rubbed together as if warming at the prospect of mischief. I visited my head right where my mother's breasts pressed against the glass pane that separated us, and sucked, all the while tears streaming down my contorted actor's face.

They asked me to speak to young men in a correctional facility, who could believe that! Even Mr Mastermind was rendered speechless and without retort by the severe, fitting irony of it.

Guards escorted me gently out of my hole and stood standing outside the stall watching me as I stepped out of my uniform and put on a blue workshirt and some jeans.

Then they drove me to the facility. The motion of the wheels underneath almost made me want to puke. And the sky outside the windows was one undifferentiated shade of blue. A blue so clean it made my teeth ache. It seemed like one more of freedom's teases and taunts.

When we got there I was shocked by the beauty of the place. It seemed a kind of perversity, as if the inhabitants were being rewarded for their delinquence, encouraged to remain in their infantilized, bad-boy states, why not just put them up at the fucking Four Seasons for heaven's sake, I said to myself. Seeing the exterior, and even more the immaculate, green-carpeted interior whose lobby was like a nightclub, you thought to yourself, at least I did, that the rewards of a life of irresponsibility and vandalism must be plushness and air conditioning. There was even a functional fireplace. In a landscape whose climate could not have needed it less.

I asked to see the boys' rooms. This was not part of the itinerary planned for me, but anger made me bold, and I made this request sound like an order, and what I saw turned my face even redder and made bile plunge up my throat like mercury inside a thermometer that had been dropped into boiling water.

They had individual quarters sealed off from the outside world not by iron gates held over from medieval torture chambers — like the ones used to lock us in every night — but by wooden doors with knobs that twisted open and closed freely. Each door had three hinges and they sang a song when you touched the knob, a song that went something like this: You pig, you fucking pig, each night you re-ti-yer, each night you're on fi-yer, in a stinking pig pen, We're the Holiday Inn and you're a Pig Pen, you pig, you stinking two-bit pig.

Suddenly self-conscious, I got my legs to stand straighter than two nails hammered into the floor that looked like green water. I betrayed neither myself nor the singing hinges.

They ushered me into a room where young men, what seemed like hundreds and hundreds of them, were seated on folding chairs arranged in some pattern I couldn't decode. Many were shifting audibly as if playing their butts for musical instruments. Seeing me come in, they stopped. Doors closed behind me, making a trap sound.

I stood in front of them, ushered behind a podium, and stared and stared until they became only glimmer-points in some ocean, like ten thousand souls of the dead going in and out. Panic gripped my chest. Try with hello, Mr Mastermind whispered. Hello, I told them. My voice, surprising me, held. Hello, they said back, as one unit. Nervous, I coughed into the air between us. No one reacted. I took this as a sign. I took a deep breath and then my mouth, acting independently, sputtered into a microphone that made me sound nothing like I was.

They had faces so legible it hurt to look into them. I could already foretell what awaited them on the other side.

While my lips were preaching a gospel that was pure bullshit — not that I heard myself, because I couldn't, but judging instead from the blue streaks of air issuing from my mouth — my brain was busy naming each face and inventing for it a corresponding fate. Going down the first row:

Paco the rapist.

Nestor, who looked bird-like: the perpetual gofer, and everybody's buttboy on lonely nights.

Dookie, with his innocent moon-face: petty thief, carjacker.

Mohammed: father of many but available to none, ghost outline in many photographs, followed by Where?, and that followed by silence, tears.

Chuckie Cheese: Chinatown extortionist, beater-up of old men whose mistrust of white legal concepts and their guardians — in short, whose lack of Americanness — will play to his great advantage.

Raul: dead at twenty to a drive-by.

Yakuza Rick: AIDS, gasping for the Holy Host at the over-crowded County USC facilities, while all around him nurses turn away so they can tend to those whose situations reward hope.

Lightning filled my head. All that time alone had turned my brain into something like God.

But it was the sudden realization, jerking me like a wrong turn, that this game could be played both ways — my sorry face opening itself up to a catalogue of boohoos for the boys' pleasure — that stopped me, and in the beat of this sudden stopping, I heard first one person laugh, and then another, and then another, until the whole auditorium became one big racking cough.

Several seconds of indecision followed, filled with the fear that I'd actually spoken my thoughts out loud, and then I realized that I'd actually said something funny, cracked a joke — and this too with only half a brain paying attention — so I began to unhook my shoulders from where fear had pushed them onto a level with my chin and let them ride a descending rollercoaster, seizing laughter along with everyone else.

I didn't know who in the prison system had marked me out as being the owner of podium abilities, but he would have been proud seeing me there.

How good was I? My words were spores in the air. They plugged up everyone's nostrils, making them twitch. For the boys' advisers — old men and women standing at the back and along the edges like prom chaperones and who seemed to have agreed to dress in plaid as a consolidation of their authority — this took the form of vigorously nodding in agreement. I used words like

Rehabilitation and Responsibility in the same way they'd been used for centuries before me. I leeched those words of any shadow meaning, that was what a microphone was for. I reorganized the world and now what held it in orbit was the tension between good and evil; I did this by exaggerating my criminal history — secretly to impress the boys, but for the adults' benefit, to scare these boys into reversing the downward spiral that was the ruling motion of their lives — and drew an arc between that and my present life: how far had I come, night into day. The chasm, and I, yawned.

And finally I made the kind of nine-to-five existence I detested seem like an achievement of the highest order, fingers just barely roasted by the white light of God's love.

All the while I kept thinking: You twerps you fuckers, I just don't want you infringing on my small-enough-as-it-is territory in the real world.

My head was shaved and it gave my words — silly putty though they were — a rusted, implacable quality that made the delinquents look away from me and deep into the hearts that were flopping cowardly inside their ribs. Their ears drummed with a fear that transformed the air around them into water that was slowly going in and crushing their lungs. And along with everything else their fingers were nervously twitching, as if playing invisible pianos, and seeing this, the adults winked at me and smiled the large smiles of beasts having just swallowed lunch.

*H*ERE I WAS, FALLING. I was always falling in the middle of the lunch hour. If my mother could see her boy now, would she still be laughing? My head was useless like a cabbage and out of my ears came red-colored goop that made me feel like I was being pumped for oil.

They rushed me to the clinic.

Oh man, said an orderly, who, it was clear from the gaping O his mouth shaped itself into, did not know anything. His black hands were veiny, and, seeing me, they shook like a drunk trying to fit a key into a lock. Small baby o's seemed to be coming out of his bigger O. They floated over my forehead like kisses waiting to descend.

A nurse peered in and immediately announced, Oh sweet baby Jesus what have you done to yourself? Oh honey oh honey, she repeated, and it took me a while to realize that she wasn't speaking to herself.

Something seemed to be wrong with my hands. That's where everyone was focused. One hand in particular was being touched as if it would fly off at any moment. Someone else's skin, applying pressure, resulted in music that only I could hear. This happened every time someone touched me. My skin hummed like underwater equipment. I wanted to turn my ears away. It had been a long time since anyone had been near me, and I was only now being reminded of this phenomenon, like one of the however many fucking signs of the apocalypse being ticked off a list, leaving only a handful left straining against the day of total annihilation.

I began to cry, encouraged by everyone around me. Me, with my fucking face that barely held back its neon announcement of Chink!, looked over by sobbing angels all wanting me to outlive my accident, me, I'd turned into everyone's American Top Ten!

I N THE HOSPITAL WARD, THE OLD MAN lying next to me was crying hot tears that turned directly into gas. I had never seen him anywhere before and couldn't be sure whether he wasn't just a figment of my imagination. Help me, he said.

Wasn't this supposed to be a moment of isolation and recovery? Fuck!

I ain't no nurse, I said to him.

He reached out and grabbed my hand, a sensation that felt real enough, it was the same hand I had slashed and which was now bandaged in yellowing white. He held it like a remote control and punched out a succession of commands that made my mouth sing a series of beeps of pain. By this point I knew he was real.

I feel so alone, he said dramatically, letting my hand go so he could raise both of his up to the sky in a gesture of What have I done to deserve this. My hand dropped with a thud.

It's sickening being alone in life, he said like he was Dick Clark announcing the title of a new song, trying out the words to see if they were convincing.

I didn't respond, and after a few seconds, during which all I could hear was his ragged breathing like he'd just been hefting heavy equipment, he asked, Did you hear what I said?

Mr Mastermind and my lips said in perfect unison: Who didn't.

Well?

Well what. Leave me alone.

Aren't you tired of being in prison?

I didn't reply.

I'm scared. Dying like this. All alone with no one, not even a stranger to cry for me.

I won't cry for you that's for sure, said my brain. But to him, to shut him up, I said, You're not dying.

How would you know? he snapped.

What do you have anyway?

I don't have to have anything, I'm an old man.

Boo hoo hoo.

You young people! He shook one comic fist at me.

I again insisted: I want to be alone.

Thank you Ms Greta Garbo, he cackled.

Leave me alone fuckhead.

There'll be plenty of time for that later on.

Just when I thought peace was settling, he announced, I've

been here twenty years. I've done my time. Why don't they let me go? Look at me. What could this body do now? Look at it. I'm an old man. Why do they keep me locked up?

Curiosity got the better of me, and I asked, What got you in here?

Murder, he replied. But look at me now.

Who'd you kill?

Many people. Before you were born. Many many people. A long line of them I killed because they were in my way and who could see the light with them blocking the view. And their mouths. They said so many things that made me feel so small. And small became smaller until I was unseen. And in the end it was what I had to do. I had to do it. There was no other choice left. I pushed them out of the way. That's what I did. And they didn't cry, not a single peep, I was so quick. And I thought, after I did it I thought, Who could ever catch me now, the invisible man? He was quiet for a moment, surprised by his confession, and then, turning to me, asked, How about you?

I killed someone too. Like him, I seemed to have volunteered information despite myself.

Between two murderers there exists the clarity of a radio signal beamed out and perfectly received. This declaration erased previous murk. We grew quiet. The old man kept his face on mine, taking a long, hard look, as if trying to foretell something. From this gesture I knew that he didn't believe in the possibility of my salvation and was only doing the next best thing: memorizing the set of my features, so he could, at a later date that was sure to come — pointing at my face's facsimile on some TV crime broadcast — brag and say, I knew that guy once.

I said to him, apropos of his earlier announcements, I'm a sharper person when alone.

As opposed to with a girl? he said, and in the saying of this, revealed himself to be a soft-hearted person who would indeed one day die alone.

As opposed to with anyone, I clarified.

Family? he asked.

Family, anyone. I'm sharper alone, I repeated.

I'm not, he replied.

And I like being sharp. I do. I really do, I said, as if afraid my point would evaporate if I didn't repeat it three times, like a magician's incantation, or the chorus of some song someone has composed to counter heartbreak.

I CLEANED THE TOILETS, was assigned to do this — mop until piss stains disappeared and scrub clean the tiles in the shower stalls and brush away watermark rings inside toilet bowls — at least once a week. Sometimes besides piss and shit, there'd be vomit. And even worse was blood. It seemed we were forever leaking necessary things. On certain days I couldn't get enough sleep. I didn't know how to whistle. Every once in a while, I'd sing in a low murmur while mopping the floor.

I worked out. I lifted weights, and didn't so much bulk up as tightened. I huffed and groaned till I could no longer endure lifting the damn things, then I'd stop, that would be how I knew to quit. What began as fifteen-minute sessions every day turned into two hours by the end of three years.

I helped fix things. I even repaired the television set which barked when back in order. My hands, once slashed, seemed to have turned miraculous.

They put us to work making small innocuous things which, to this day, I have no idea what they were. They seemed the brains for toys, small gadgets that had screws requiring tightening. That's what I did: I screwed and screwed, building a mountain, and at the end of the day, someone would come and sweep my work into a big laundry basket to take to some place only he knew about and my table would turn empty, as if I'd spent the whole day doing nothing.

The prison had a room where they threw old newspapers and magazines into piles that stood floor to ceiling. I went there a lot, followed by no one, and no one ahead of me. I was first in line for the day's papers, beating even the guards, and always leafed past important shit to get to the obituaries. I read and read, as if in these people's lives — whole buildings reduced to the rubble of sorrows and accomplishments — I could glean some secret with which to console myself, or prevent the very same things happening to me, not the success part, which I was in no danger of, but the sorrows.

In the beginning, I also scoured profiles of successful people, athletes and rock singers and entrepreneurs, particularly if these were accompanied by smiling, colored photographs of the subjects posed in environments related to, or brought about by, their success, such as beautiful homes, or the basketball courts on which their preeminence was established. And then later, when it dawned on me that this was exactly like taking poison, I stopped.

There was a large yard surrounded by chainlink that was topped by circular knots of razor wire which they'd push us out to, to benefit I guess from the heat and the toxic sunlight. I'd go if I felt like it, even though in theory this was mandatory, and stare and stare at a boy named Alex Marquez, who was fifteen and owned a face that mystified me. He didn't inspire any of the standard feelings, neither anger nor lust, nor did he remind me of myself, or of anyone else I'd ever encountered in my life, he simply looked like a mystery, and into his face would slide probabilities and scenarios that, once having sunk in, would never surface again for me to know if they were a perfect match or merely extensions of my fancy.

I stared at him surreptitiously, and then when I realized he didn't care one way or another, wasn't at all embarrassed by what the others would think about me, us, I looked with even greater intensity, out in the open. Everyone held their breaths. But not once did he acknowledge my stares. We were as solitary and separate as we'd been even after three years of being in the same place. What was it about that face? He wasn't even good-looking. He had acne spraying up and down both jawlines and above his chin; hair that he obviously didn't care for; and dead eyes like that of an old man, cataracted. Was it that? The incongruous marriage of his being fifteen and having the admirable poker-face of the elderly?

He came up to me once. He walked in a straight line whose end point could only have been me. My heart beat savagely, like a countdown to something gigantic. But it turned out that when he got to me I had to move out of his way. He was going to the rec room to join in the other men's chorus of laughter. The air took on an oppressiveness, like curtains falling over a bright window.

EVERYTHING WAS CHANGING, but changing in ways that represented somebody else's victory.

My favorite song, for instance, was no longer my favorite song. There was no new favorite to supplant the old one. It had died just like that, in prison. One afternoon, lying on my cot, I heard the old favorite coming out of someone's radio and realized it was no longer my favorite, that was how I knew. I danced with several boys to this song, in another life. Every beat of it was a directive for the hips to move first forward, then back, then sideways, and then it invited the ass to participate, first the left, then the right, over and over until you came up with something that, in the nature of most dances, looked like fucking. This song, and the dance it inspired, was a corroboration of how young people viewed the world: danger and immortality a finger-length away, unlockable with that first key: sex. If they could accomplish that, then everything else would unfurl and spill out before them. I no longer thought about that, except as a dim joke on my past.

One day I visited the prison's barbershop, which was not a barbershop at all but a small, windowless room with one of the guards standing in the center. He manned a single chair in the very middle of the room, standing to the left like a potted plant next to a throne. Clenched in his fist, as if a weapon, was a stainless steel razor that buzzed and buzzed. The room didn't have mirrors, everything about it was makeshift. It was a place the prison opened only once a week for us, to help manage a recent infestation of head lice. The rest of the week it just sat there, locked up and mysterious.

I sat in the chair. He pushed my head back and, starting from the nape, worked upwards, in clean strokes. He didn't say a word, and neither did I, I didn't have to, because there was only one cut possible, which was a complete buzz. I felt like I was being tickled, but suppressed any hint of laughter. There is nothing, I thought to myself, more insulting to these people than laughter. He swept through my back, then turning to face me, worked on the front, in a style that minimized the chance of contact. The machine's buzz filled my ears. I stared at his chest, and when that made me uncomfortable I looked down at his shoes, black patent leather lace-ups he'd recently had shined, so vigorously in fact that a vaporous version of my face stared back at me. In his hands the instrument was like a washcloth, wiping up and down. Hair fell all around me, puddling around my feet.

All that I'd had saved was of no use to me now. What would protect me in this world? Nothing. I was naked and would have to put meanness on my face to talk to people.

I felt hair come down on my face, dawdling on my small nose, my lips, before dropping. And when it dropped it made a small rustling sound, like something irretrievable, a fork raking regretfully over the tight surface of a drum, like in jazz.

THE WRIST-SLASHING YANKED ME DOWN. Not even pity worked in my favor. Guard eyes, scanning my face and figure to head off another attack, broadcast to one other as soon as something suspicious loomed. And, unbeknownst to me, it did. A rake for the outside yard was pulled from my hands. As this happened people looked. Many were noticing me for the first time. I'd volunteered for yard duty, thinking this would raise my brownie-point tally back to where it had been before the suicide attempt, but instead they took the rake from my hands. Clean up the toilets instead was the order given me. I was back to my old job. A mop and bucket, and a washcloth and soap: these were my permanent instruments now. Nothing sharp to slice open skin or to impale myself on.

Everything I did radiated with the possibility of mishap, and once more I felt like I was in the role intended for me right from birth, cast according to skill: the bad seed. And this sped the time. It revivified me. I knew my enemy once more and, knowing, plotted, Mr Mastermind stroking me back to health.

I became nice to the guards. It was part of the plan.

Even the priest was a beneficiary. Once a month this man came to counsel his flock, unwaywarding them. Once a month, seeing him, I put on blind eyes and shuffled to a rhythm that made me unapproachable. He asked about me, that much I knew. When apprised of my name, he knitted his brows. It was as if from my name came forth an encyclopedia of bad information that made his heart beat faster. But I knew he was as stupid as the rest.

One day I approached him, finally letting him have that pleasure. He was taken aback. Surprise knocked a hole into his features, into which I beamed and beamed. I let him touch my hand.

I let him put his filthy paws on my forehead like a rape. It was all part of The Plan. Rehabilitation: a chorus of angels would sing, unfurling that very word in a banner over my head. Meanwhile their angel-assholes would fart God's blessing everywhere. I continued to let this man stroke my hands. Even when his calluses raked a river-line into my palms I said nothing.

I whispered into this priest's ear: Father.

My life, looking back on it now, seemed full of fathers. Even their absence was an imprint.

Father, I said to him, I want to get better. This was a line rescued from my past, but herded away from earnestness — which could lead to nothing but ruin, as my life had proven — and turned towards a sharper light, metal-like, I was using it now to deceive, avenge having been sold a bill of worthless goods: that the society of normal people were reserving a place for me, waiting and waiting only for me to get better to join them. Hah!

Father, I said to this man, I want to get better. Our intimacy, unmediated by the screen of any confessional, made him shiver. He made the sign of the cross, touching points on his face and body that, through constant practice, had finger-grooves on them. And he smiled. Which was exactly what I knew he would do. And inwardly I smiled back, my yellow teeth turning into fangs. Father, help me. Again he smiled. He meant to show kindness, but a smug contentment shone forth instead. This man had cellophane for skin, he could hide nothing, he was my puppet.

He began to say the things his profession had equipped him to say, in tones cultivated not to arouse suspicion. These were the words that he laid down between us, like cards, which I put on a show of accepting: Forgiveness. Clemency. (Weren't they the goddamn same word? I said to myself, irritated. But after all, I reminded myself, these people love redundancy.) Afterlife. Whiteness. Sincerity. Daily. Struggle. Prayer. Forgiveness, he repeated, emphasizing his position of centrality, and here I had to suppress another groan. Self-love. Catholicism. Papal. (Papal? I mimicked, turning my eyes to the ceiling. I improvised: I bet the motherfucker's constipated! I made this comment to the vaudeville audience inside my head, who appeared like uniform rows of plants: short men wearing green suits, bow ties and, atop their flat heads, straw hats. Papal? I repeated, and this audience, not having gotten enough, guffawed until they dropped to their knees, slapping the floor.) Communion, the priest continued. Worthy. Mass. Scripture. Guidance. Whiteness, he repeated. (Fat chance, Mr Mastermind said in retort to this.) Sin. Fight. Success. Absolution. Reward. Heaven!

That's the word he chose to close with — heaven with both eyelids shut and fluttering as if tranced — and he said it in an arrogant voice perfectly in line with the pop-star rays I saw emanating from his chest. Heaven to each of us meant something different. I did not share the pearly white vision of his child's belief. Our disagreement met somewhere in the middle and clashed noisily like animals with shells. Mine, the darker, more clawed thing, won.

The man had white hair, and a white ring around his neck that seemed like a noose, turning his oily face red. He wiped his brow with a handkerchief that smelled of a woman's hand: detergent and ironing. Was this man married? I looked at his finger. He owned no jewelry.

I said all the right things. Mainly I said Yes. I felt like the boys I'd preached to, subintelligent. I said Yes again and again, and like Ali Baba, for each one I was rewarded with his mouth opening, revealing beautiful teeth.

Afterwards, he reported my behavior to the parole board. You have a good boy in jail, he testified to them into a microphone, as they sat before him like a horizontal panel of beauty contest judges, stern and with frozen smiles flashed at just the right juncture. Thank you father, they told him. When he was dismissed, they conferred among themselves, talking like every crowd scene of every film in the world put together on an endless loop, before reaching a decision that was unanimous: Let the boy go. He deserves another chance.

I picked another sucker for my plans, an inmate named Luzon Ybanes who got in by killing his family. He was a Filipino and had a face as far from Alex Marquez as it was possible to have. This was a sign for me. I looked at him one day and thought, I'm picking you. And I did, I picked him, making sure to turn any kindness I showed him into great theater. Elders saw us and smiled. Two Asians in a common fellowship. Many such geek stories had been attributed to me before, and now came time to extract revenge. Seeing me do a playlet called The Brotherhood of Man, the guards relayed news, I'm sure, backwards down a line until it led to the authorities who would release me.

I said so many stupid things to this stupid boy, and he, having only wanted someone to befriend him in prison, smiled the heart-rending smile of the innocent. I said: God sent me. I said: My heart goes out to you. What was going on inside this boy's mouth? I tried to look past the little hanging waddle at the back of his teeth and into his throat every time he opened his mouth. Blood pumped extra hard to the inside of this place, turning it crimson with gratitude and hopefulness.

I N THE YARD WE HUDDLED next to each other, rubbing our palms together, and even as I looked at Alex Marquez, I pretended that all my attention, the sharp bright laser of my friendship, was focused on Luzon, and on him alone. He confessed to me about his family, how much he'd hated them, their Catholic strictures and how they'd forbid him to go out on the weekends, and given him a curfew on weekday nights. What is this? he'd told them. Martial law? Who are you? Marcos? He laughed. Get it? he asked me, slapping me on the knee. I slapped back.

He had a jovial air that belied his being a killer of family. But come to think of it, who in this place didn't?

He told me his dreams, and though this was too much to take, I egged him on.

In his conversations he was reflecting one of the past selves I had no desire to be reunited with. This past self was a gangly scarecrow of humiliation. I could hardly breathe. He said that he wanted to be normal. That's the word he used. Twinning him with a life I'd tried to put behind me. Laughter the most subversive thing in the world, I reminded myself, and kept my true emotions hidden. Actually I was torn between laughing and crying. I want to be normal, he again insisted. He brushed sandy hair from his forehead and brought his face down onto two hands that awaited like a pillow. He buried himself and sobbed. This was a moment devised to test me: Would I take my act far enough? I did. I took him into my arms and, with the guard's permission, walked him to the infirmary. I held his hand.

In bed, he persisted. He repeated to me, I want to be normal. The nurses smiled.

And that wasn't the worst of it. Normality for him had a specific cast, he knew exactly what it looked like, its very smell, and he couldn't wait to share it with me: He wanted to own a hardware store, as an uncle of his had done in the Philippines. In Bicolod, to be exact. That name made me visualize insects gumming leaves between their mandibles.

He wanted to go back home and open a hardware store to which he would attach his family's name, as penance. Seeing his family's name writ large he'd be reminded every day. He needed to be reminded. A true Catholic, I said to myself, laughing all the while the laugh of Mr Mastermind, who added: As if anyone could escape reminding.

Or, said Luzon, I'd like to own a McDonald's. Feed my people good food.

Your people? I asked him, thinking he was referring to family, in which case his dreams didn't make sense: hadn't he killed them all?

My people, he said, clarifying: The Filipinos. I want them to know what truly good food is.

Oy, said my head, and in my imagination I slapped a palm onto my forehead.

Meanwhile, all Luzon saw were my features arranged into an imitation of the Virgin Mary's, placid, but with a depth charge of sorrow imploding somewhere behind my skin, compassionate. He said, as he kneaded my hand into the mattress, I thank God for you.

And what was I thinking? I saw all the tomorrows of my world changed by this benign play-acting, all the tomorrows of my world framed by doors that squeaked open with the slightest breeze.

RAUL THE RAPIST. OR WAS IT PACO? Anyhow, him: that first boy sitting in the front row at the correctional facility, the one whose group I'd preached to. He came to our prison one day. He stepped through the big doors. Was this his turn to visit, as it had been mine weeks back? I asked myself, before one of the guards — one of the two who accompanied me to the boys' facility — filled me in on the whole sordid story: He'd knifed another boy seventeen times during a fight and killed him, into the face as well as the heart, seventeen stab wounds all in all, that was why he was here. Would this be the fate of everything I touched? How many other boys were going to come in with my track record flashing on their faces? This one was in for life. And his true name was neither Paco nor Raul. It was Tommee.

Tommee with an ee, said the guard. I avoided him everywhere, but flush with success he didn't even register my existence. And why should he, he was a superstar and who was I, I was only yesterday's news? Victory? Whatever, the geek speaker, reeking of fish.

What happens to your body when you grow old? Your eyes turn opaque. Your walk slows to a creep.

All this could be seen in the man who slept next to me in the hospital ward, who I named Mr Z. Z for the end of the line. I thought about him a lot. But I wouldn't go so far as to say dreamt. His song about being alone, sung expertly and with a cloud of contrition over his head like a personal spotlight, haunted me.

Because he was old and invited harming, they sequestered him from the rest, a shadow figure I always looked for and thought I saw in the corners of rooms but who always evaporated in smoke when I turned my head.

One day, he appeared in the yard. It was a beautiful summer day, a breeze blew in from the mountaintops and ruffled our shirts. It was a movie feeling transposed directly to real life. Only I noticed. Everyone else was up to their usual business, huddling in groups of private friendship.

Mr Z came over to me. He walked the slowest walk on earth, making me feel like a groom itching at the altar. When he finally drew level, Excuse me young man, was all he said, before lowering himself as if to gain a better view of my knees. He didn't need to hold any part of my body for ballast.

Wacha up to old man, I said down to him. In sunlight and back to health, his face looked different. He had deep grooves on his forehead like ink stains, and a bulbous nose that looked as if it had been on the receiving end of a pummeling machine.

What? he asked. It turned out he didn't even recognize me, I was only standing next to a spot by the chainlink that he'd wanted.

I reintroduced myself.

Oh my God, he said. So you are. He unbuttoned the top buttons of his shirt and cracked his neck. It made a machine sound that reminded me of getting my haircut.

How are you? I asked him.

I'm old, he replied.

Oh no not that chorus again.

And yourself young man?

I'm fine, I replied, lying.

Are you better? he asked, moving his head to indicate my wrist.

I got a scar, I replied, but otherwise I'm fine.

Can I see it?

My scar?

May I see your scar?

Sure. I lowered myself to him and stretched out my hand.

He held it like a piece of fruit, afraid to bruise it. That's a nice scar, he said.

I don't know why I did it, I confessed.

Because you were tired.

And I replied, I've been tired so many times before why now?

Cumulative, he explained. It takes its toll. You have family?

My mother.

That's it?

Me and my mother, that's it.

I have two children, he confessed.

Oh yeah?

Two boys.

Where are they now?

In prison, he replied. He didn't flinch. Nothing changed in his attitude as he said this.

Both of them?

Well. One of them's dead, the other's still in prison.

Is he here? I asked, thinking that that would have been fantastical — a father and son in the same prison, two lives led as one — and yet, not really, stranger things have happened, were happening every day around us.

No, replied Mr Z. He's in Utah.

Did he kill someone too? I asked, then immediately apologized by saying, Listen old man if you think I should shut up I will cause it's really none of my business.

No no, he replied. You're curious. I would be too. It's good. To reach my age. You want to talk about it. He said this to me: Suffering reborn as story. No, he said of his son, he didn't kill someone. He tried to. But he didn't succeed.

How old is he?

I lost count, Mr Z replied. How old are you?

The answer took me a few seconds to recall. Twenty-eight, I told him. Wait, I said almost as immediately, twenty-nine. Either twenty-eight or twenty-nine, I'm not sure which.

Will you get out of here in time to take advantage of your youth? he asked.

This was what I wanted to say: I think so.

But some paranoid switch inside me turned on. Probably with the help of Mr Mastermind, who said: Don't let on. Don't jinx yourself by bragging. So instead I told Mr Z, I don't know.

It'd be a pity if you didn't, he said. Look at me.

After a moment's silence, he announced, Your mother must love you a lot.

What makes you say that?

I love my boys. I miss them.

And I tried to think whether this was true or not: Did she, my mother, love me? Small things I could marshal as evidence in her favor. The way she'd sing to me as a boy, things like that. Did that constitute love? She was an inarticulate woman, no declaration of affection ever crossed those lips. And she hit me. Disappointment made her do this. Cumulative. That was the word. We stitched and stitched, collecting whatever pieces were close at hand, and in the end a blanket of hate, the color of smog, sat in our hands to surprise us.

Did this woman love me? She never drank, never took drugs, never fooled around. She'd never fallen in love, as far as I could tell. My father was for her an arranged marriage. Because of this she never grew into a woman who could understand the necessity of jeans with holes cut in strategic places. Or hair that looked like you didn't care, when in fact you cared a lot. Or how the closeness of someone's skin can make you forget if you were a boy or a girl; forget where you were born, that you'd just come from another country and that this was supposed to be the center of everything, where fear and superstition would radiate outwards to contaminate every part of your life; next to that skin, those lips, everything looked like a blackboard eraser had just been through with them.

My mother used to live in Thailand, a green, foodless place. Now she lives in the States, in Los Angeles, that pancake city of dread. In neither place does her spirit live. Where it thrives is on that bridge between both, the one she crossed in the middle of her fortieth year, each arm ending in a suitcase packed quickly and tight. The weight of those things still pull her hands down. Could a woman like this love? Could a woman who was neither future nor present tense marshal enough energy to notice a child growing twisted like some reverse metamorphosis of butterfly into caterpillar, into worm, and once noticing, throw in copious amounts of something to counter it? Could life for this woman be anything but too late?

One day, when she came to visit, I said into the phone, looking at her, I said, Mom you look so pretty today. And you could tell she was nonplussed. You could follow that look in her eyes all the way to some place entitled What Might Have Been, all the way back and back to Thailand, receding in the speed of light.

Mr Z loved his boys. They lived in Utah, some place by the sound of its name I know I will never be. Mr Z pumped gas, fixed cars. All this I imagined him doing under a rusted Texaco sign that creaked and creaked to announce wind, the onset of spring.

When time allowed, he took his boys in his truck, and they went driving through countryside that was as flat and burnt-out as a penny. He taught his boys the difference between a fox and a jackal. From him they learned the pleasure derivable from the steady positioning of the barrel capped off by the squeeze of the trigger. And then, in time, when his bloodthirst demanded more, he worked on humans. Mr Z killed and killed. He was a man who knew what it was like to fall backwards.

Only a man like that could have it in him — his will like a pestle and mortar working day and night — to love me. And love me with the only love I'll ever be comfortable with: something ringed on the outside by caution and whose center did not have a heat so hot as to require the constant upkeep of fulfilled expectations. Only a man like that who, having disappointed so many others, was careful in his turn not to expect much of anyone, even his sons, of whom I could be one. Only a man like that and nobody else.

WHO PUT THE JUH IN JOKE? This person entertained irony long enough to put the very same sound in joy.

Work release began. Hah! And I thought I'd be released without further ado.

Twice a week they drove me to a Korean grocer's where first I was a stockboy and then, when the proprietor's children were on vacation, a cashier.

The proprietor's wife watched me with eyes that screamed to be let out of their sockets, so they could follow me wherever I went. Behind her back I muttered the name I convinced myself she was born with: Robotwoman.

Robotwoman spoke poor English. Her husband, who I found spookily quiet, turned out to speak none. In her mouth words sounded mushed together and made up. Immediately this set things up.

You can say tell me how much and I can say punching on cash register and you can see how is like to make change-ah for customer person, she said by way of introduction.

Oh God, I sighed, do I have to spend more time with my mother and her tribe?

The children were sufficiently indifferent to this new person hovering around their parents' store to make me yearn for prison instead. Already I was filled with the conviction that this was a preview, a warning of the real life that awaited me on release.

There were two of them, a son and a daughter, and both their faces already had a look in them of heading out the door without turning back. They could speak English to begin with, and resented having to translate for their parents day and night. And I'm sure they had friends with busy lives that made theirs seem at best some watery carbon, and this more than anything made them dream their parents' death every night.

The boy was seventeen, eighteen, and the girl a year younger. She looked at me one day. She stared and then kept staring some more. Even when I let her know I knew what she was doing she didn't stop. She wasn't shy. But we never transacted. Maybe she didn't think I could speak English and so hesitated to start anything. I had very little occasion to open my mouth in the store, and when I did barely a sound came out before I was cut off by Robotwoman. Already the daughter was growing enormous breasts, and you could tell that trouble was just beginning to stretch its mischievous fingers.

*I*N THE STORE THERE WERE SPECIFIC DAYS when business slowed. I can't remember what these were, but they were always, without fail, the same days. Some clock held sway over the neighborhood that we catered to.

Robotwoman and I were watching TV on one of these days. We were just sitting there watching Kung Fu.

In prison the program of choice was a cops and robbers show shot with a handheld camera, called Those Men In Blue. Everyone guffawed watching the cops put on their macho act — driving funny cars and speaking into pretend walkie-talkies — and they grunted when confronted with images of criminals that had nothing to do with them: either meek like sissies or impudent but inept like drunken punks. Outrage filled the room and converged, rising as a poison cloud, only to be diffused in bursts of violent, sustained laughter.

Robotwoman chewed her gum, making a sound like an electric appliance. People looked at her askance wherever she went, and their handshakes and nervous titters were formed by the things we were watching on TV, things like karate chops and the groundward glance of eyes painted sloelike, but she only concentrated on the gum inside her mouth, and for her that was what was important. From Korea to gum. Story of a journey, completed.

In dreams, I was never once haunted by the man who I'd shot. He was dead. That was that. A deserved end, with me chosen by natural law to deal it. That was that.

The magazines I continued to read had pictures of couple after couple, which I bypassed. I didn't want to look. How could so much be purported to have changed and people still be kissing? My lips were flat and dry.

I looked in the mirror when I went to take a shower, and only then, seeing my face, was I reminded of God. God who are you and why do you hate me so much? My ugliness was so specific there was no other question to ask.

I caught Tommee and Alex Marquez talking one day. I had to do a doubletake to make sure my eyes weren't playing a trick. There they were, conferencing by the mess door. When they saw me, they feigned nonchalance. Were they talking about me? What could they be saying? They had me in common, after all. What had happened to turn them into fast friends? They were both teenagers, for one, emitting that stupid, hungry look of being untouched by either heartbreak or backbreaking work. I decided that was it. While all around them, the faces took on the shared experience of a bygone generation that creaked and grimaced with barely held-in pain and failure, they found and clung to each other in fear.

Luzon Ybanes, seeing me alone at mealtime, came and sat down. The loss of both Alex and Tommee's friendship, added to this, became too much to take. But I'd tamed him, turned him into some pet, and for this I deserved not to be given a moment's peace. No no, it was going too far.

I want to be alone, I told him.

And without saying a word, he took his tray elsewhere.

On work release, I found myself lying on grass that circled a big tree, and staring up at the sky. The clouds were clouds. They were not elephants, or boats, or a housewife preparing dinner. They were clouds. It had been a long time since I'd seen so many. Like me, they were no longer slashed apart by bars or chainlink or razor wire.

But this was only recess.

Meanwhile, the grocery store hummed the fucking hum of my absence.

TRYING TO EXPEDITE MY RELEASE, I decided to turn friendly to Luzon Ybanes once again. I talked to him about the proprietors' daughter, who I called Cynthia. That wasn't her name but it was what I called her. Just as Robotwoman was Robotwoman, Cythia became Cynthia. Luzon wanted to know all about work release. What's it like? he asked, his earnest face tipped back into the cold shadows. He was warming himself with the fantasy of being able to touch the outside world. I told him about Cynthia, the most vivid thing of the outside world. Ooo eee, he reacted, and then he started touching himself. He didn't think that I could see him.

Good morning little schoolgirl, sang Van Morrison one day, and I picked it as her theme song: Good morning little schoolgirl, I sang to her beautiful back which was shaped like a violin. Stacking cans one by one in an order that, were anybody looking, would reveal my great fear of not being up to snuff, I continued to sing that song. I wanted Cynthia to hear.

What you say doing? Robotwoman barked at me.

Nothing nothing, I replied.

You making quickly no say no singing that silly very silly, she admonished.

Yes ma'am, I told her.

Cynthia came out of the stockroom and, choosing a circuitous route to the register, brushed against me.

Good morning little schoolgirl, I sang towards her bra straps, which I could see beneath her transparent jersey. They looked designed to fall.

She smiled, even while her mother looked on, disbelieving. When she reached the counter, a slap fell on Cynthia's shoulders.

Ow, said Cynthia, adjusting her bra straps.

Good morning little schoolgirl, I sang to console her.

Cynthia smiled.

You, Robotwoman pointed at me like a dog. You no say singing that anymore or else you say have yourself out of a job-job.

Yes ma'am, I replied, smirking. Only Cynthia understood. My

sense of irony was another level of English that eluded
Robotwoman.

Finally she let me touch her breasts. I smiled, and my smile,
like everything else about me when I was with her, was throw-
away, regal in its confidence. Because she was good, a good girl in
line with all the other good girls of the world who belonged to
good immigrant parents from good countries, she had to come
and find me.

Luzon, needing solace one night, asked me about Cynthia
some more. He had a black eye given to him apparently by
Tommee and Alex. They'd settled on him as the one. I could imagine why. Luzon, ever since his conversion, walked like a victim,
meek and full of the sunshine of life. So they'd cornered him in the
showers and beat him up. Apparently they'd heard that Normal
was his mantra, and sought to turn their derision into action.

Now all he wanted to do was listen to stories of my work release
to inspire him to leave. Or to stockpile his anger, and thus pumped
up, take revenge on Tommee and Alex. I looked at his clothes but
couldn't detect anything concealed underneath them, so I took it for
granted that he was just making an empty threat. He wanted to be
reminded of the things he was being deprived of, he said.

So I told him about Cynthia's breasts. I pinched them. And she
threw her head back, moaning. She pushed my head down and let
me knead her chest with my lips. I didn't tell Luzon that all the
time I was doing this, even when I put a finger in her and slid in
and out, all I was thinking of were the boys in my life with their
various heads stuck onto one gigantic, writhing, monstrous body,
a beast frightened townspeople pointed to and called Desertion.

*I*T WAS NIGHT. Somebody's pocket radio was emitting big
band music. I couldn't tell how many cells down from me
this was. And behind it was the faint but unmistakable sound of

someone getting beaten up.

My mother appeared. She was falling in love. She told me this. And then the man she'd fallen in love with also appeared. They started dancing to the sound of the big band music, this song which was sad and beautiful at the same time, unbearably so. She wore a kind of flimsy nightgown common to movie women. She smiled. On her face joy looked incongruous, like a newborn's wrinkled countenance. I pushed my head to the wall and willed myself deaf. Immediately she stopped dancing and disappeared.

I thought of Cynthia: My talent for love would have to look elsewhere.

I no longer mourned the distance between myself and the two boys who beat up my ward. Tommee and Alex, who continued beating Luzon up. Maybe that was them working right now, under cover of soft music, fisting into skin. He wore his bruises like a collection, this Luzon. His face puffed and deflated, like a fish, over and over again. Seeing him it was all I could do to keep from laughing. When I started avoiding him he must have finally known my true face.

Work release gave me so many more friendships to aspire to anyway. Robotwoman's son was not one of these, however. He looked at me with a disdain he was wise to check with fear. Money would find this boy in a few years, you could tell, and more importantly, it would stay with him. He had a fat body that a suit would turn charismatic. And every day I was at their store was a day when my thinness sent a rebuke to the one thing he felt crippled by, his appearance. No wonder he hated me.

I continued stacking cans and punching the buttons on the cash register like a boxing match, releasing the cash box with a ring whose novelty very quickly wore off. I carried heavy boxes from delivery trucks to the storage room. I could feel muscles multiplying underneath my shirt. But everything was beginning to turn a yellow that was like the color of my hopes petrifying. When would I ever be free? It was killing me to have to be on my best behavior every day. I could feel my guts and my veins constricting at the effort. The routine of work release was like a new imprisonment.

Then it happened.

Luzon Ybanes, escaping from his own work release, came into my store, the store where I worked, holding a gun. He didn't know I worked there. He didn't know anything except that the contents of the cash register needed freeing. He sought to restore the order of things, and with a gun there was no unpersuading him.

I happened to be in the back.

Empty that fucking cash register, he barked to Robotwoman, whose face bore no sign of either panic or fear. For once, her estrangement from English worked to her advantage.

I heard everything as if through layers of water and, curious, came out. And there I saw him. Was this the same man who shrieked Normal! one day at the top of his lungs and made me think he was requesting a drug, the one who'd turned my face white with embarrassment? Maybe after all, every time I thought I was using him, he was really using me; he wanted to be put on work release and, escaping, find his way here. It boggled my mind to think that life had this in store all along: a minor character takes the reigns. Even heroism would choose someone not my friend to update its face, wasn't that the story of my life! — someone who, if you asked me, I would tell you wasn't worth betting on in the scheme of things, much less to think about betting on, not in a million years: a fucking Filipino! McDonald's, hah! Now I could see it in the bright light of its shamhood. He, too, it turned out, had a Mr Mastermind working for him. Only his was much smarter than the one barking orders to my nerve ends and muscles.

His new face was set in stone. Sweat did several ski trails down it. They collected at his nose, dropping as one huge balloon of liquid. You could hear it plop it was so quiet.

Give me the fucking money, he ordered again.

Robotwoman reached towards where the register was. Luzon, hearing the sudden giveaway of my sneakers, turned. And he saw me then. That was how he died: looking at me. Underneath the register, it turned out, Robotwoman kept a gun. I didn't know this. I knew nothing, and couldn't scream. I stood there as if within the rubber-cement confines of a nightmare. He looked. I stared. And then, capping our mutual shock of recognition, before I could even call out his name, or him undo the question mark on his face, Luzon's head came flying to one corner, while his body dropped straight to the ground. Robotwoman screamed. She screamed first for herself, and then for the both of us. My open mouth made no sound.

T HESE ARE NAMES THAT I WILL TRY TO FORGET, but which will never desert me: Luzon. Bicolod. McDonald's. Alex Marquez. Tommee/Raul/Paco. Mr Z. Utah. Cynthia. Korea.

On again, off again, on lonely nights.

The day of release was a day made dull by repetition in dreams. I'd been thinking about it so much that now that it was finally here, I couldn't feel a thing. But I knew this: I was leaving them all behind.

The keys they used to open one set of bars made a sound like musical bells but when I looked at the guards who were escorting me out their faces were stoic. Could it be that they expected me back and so were reserving their congratulations for someone else?

Everyone I was leaving behind would soon be dead and their deaths would not be honored, not even cursorily, by an obituary. I would never read about them. Luzon was one. He will sink into stone, foundation for another generation. In years to come, although I will forget exactly who this group held, an essence of this, of being passed by, will always remain with me. It will shriek its birdcall inside my chest when I'm in airports and bus terminals, anyplace where I'm moving away from something stationary and it recedes and recedes from vision until finally it passes into haunting.

I will seek out Mr Z's boy, the one in prison in Utah, I promised myself. I will make sure to tell him about his father, who has charged me with remembering.

I lied to my mother about today, and she was nowhere to be found. The money she'd sent in the mail was in my shirt pocket. Four hundred dollars. I had never had so much money at one time in my life.

The guards patted me down.

My sneakers were new ones, given to me as metaphors by the prison system. They squeaked as they led me out to a waiting car. Burning all around us was the brilliant white light of a drug overdose, blinding with the fire of a former life screaming, Don't forget me, don't you ever outlive me.

At the park, children. So many boys guardrailed against harm by the fingers of loving parents. Would I ever get a share in this? Watching them made me violent and thirsty. I bought a Coke. It seemed a great luxury to be able to do this. Just sit, and by the drinking of a Coke declare oneself the owner of a history parallel to everyone else's.

My mind fixed on the word thirsty. And then, with the giddiness of too much freedom, thirsty became thirty. I was thirty. When had I turned? I didn't remember, but nonetheless there it was facing me: I was thirty. Thirty! I touched my head. I felt my wrist for the scar, which was growing more imperceptible with each day. I tried out the word Normal on my lips, and decided it wouldn't fit. I had to find some other. None that the priest gave me, that was for sure. Except maybe striving. It promised, but was careful not to promise too much.

Extemporaneous speech once glinted off my body with the sheen of new dimes. Looking at me, could these people tell? I've spoken to boys, junior versions of myself I tried to rescue, a rare good deed. I've touched my own past in the form of these boys, and tried to reroute them towards a light, some sight I wasn't used to. I would be meeting them again in this world, I was sure, one by one dressed in newly pressed shirts and pants, and they would be like a procession of totems assuring me of my usefulness. Could people tell? I never killed a man over anything like the contents of a cash register. I stood innocent, solitary. Could people tell from my face, the way I held myself? Could they give me that at least?

My hands, those talented things, ached for hard, gainful employment. These are things that could save me, I thought looking down at them, and the thought of it warmed me.

There would be so many things later.

I would be turned down again and again by boardinghouses that I, in the hopes of giving myself a fresh start, would visit. They would find me unsuitable for different reasons, all of them made up. The only one that would take me in would give me a room with windows that had stone-shattered holes in their center, where the wind would suck in and out like a terminal patient. It would have cockroaches too. At night they would roll across the floor like eightballs expertly struck. And because of this I would never be able to save any food I'd bought. I would also stare up at a ceiling from which a fan had been yanked, where the only thing remaining would be yellow stains outlining this ghost fan, stains that, on certain nights, rearranged themselves into biblical faces of torment. Add to that the soundtrack of the wind sucking in and out of those windows and I would turn into a Munch painting I'd seen again and again in reproduction. I would see it everywhere and disregard it, realizing only when it was too late that it was meant as a portent, a special message for me.

But none of this I knew as I sat on that park bench, breathing in sweet air. My head was blank and I was eager. The sun was shining. The grass green.

O UTSIDE THE PARK, bordering it in a semi-circle, was a collection of stores that looked like a fake village. A pet store was in the middle, from which issued the deafening cries of birds. At the other side of the park was a white wall on which a mural had been painted by ex-convicts, advertising their new-found Christianity. Jesus was opening both arms to welcome me, and his feet were cushioned by blue-white clouds.

What else would be awaiting me?

Several bottles of liquor. And the surprise of finding myself desirable once more. My tightened body putting me on the market for prostitution, and quickly. Shirts at the Salvation Army, with my name tattooed invisibly over their collars, waiting just for me. And several dead-end alleys and doorways providing bedding for the night when I couldn't scrounge up enough money, or was too drunk to realize I had any in my pockets. That kind of story, just so much upping and downing, like a seismographic readout looked at but not understood.

And there will be days too of magnanimousness, knowing that I could kill every fucking one of you, just like that and without exception, oh boy, the moon's a fraud and God like smeared lipstick and how many times was I burned and won't I make sure the same thing happens to you, I could kill you in not even a wink, every single one going snap like the sound of my hand leaving its perch at wrist-level, I could, but choosing to expend it all by walking aimless, agitated circles around the city instead, meeting no one's eyes.

But for now I was thirty. And it was spring! Spring was here! I'd been released into spring, a rare felicitous bit of timing. After so much teasing, spring had finally decided to stay. The wind coursed through the city, turning all the signs of all the stores into windchimes.

I got up.

I was thirty. It was the middle of spring. And I was alive. Yes, alive, while others were dead. People who, it seemed to me, had died for me, in my place. A long line of them.

The hair that I'd had shaved was starting to grow back on my boy's head. I could feel each strand reaching for the sun, like plants too long in the dark. I brushed my hand through. It felt like a breeze was blowing on my scalp. And how good it was I could not even begin to tell anyone. My mouth opened but again it made no sound.

STOMPIE

R o s e   M o s s

*I*ALMOST STEPPED ON THE CHILD'S HEAD before I saw him curled at the bottom of the stairs, the red hood of his jacket pulled over his head like a caul. He had drawn his knees up to his heart in search of a place in sleep warmer than the subway floor. I hurried on to the State House to see if I could vote in the Election the next day. I never met Stompie while he was alive, and the last thing anyone expects is to step on the face of a dead person.

*I*N THE STATE HOUSE THEY WERE SETTING UP tables for voting. The Consul talked like a bureaucrat who has worked things to a satisfactory conclusion. Even though I am an American citizen now, I could come back and vote the next day. For this Election they were making up the rules. I could live in two countries, beyond history and division, as though we were already in the ultimate state of the soul. For one day, the world in which I live far from where I was born would be one world, and I could live like a suturing needle flying to and fro.

The Consul wanted documents to show who I am, so I showed my birth certificate. If I had come with no papers at all — if I had crossed a river of crocodiles and a reserve of lions — he would have accepted an affidavit. But I came to Boston years ago without trouble. The Consul wanted to hold onto my birth certificate. Perhaps he would take it to his expensive hotel to fax New York or Pretoria and ask who I really am.

Leaving the State House I walked down the granite steps and into the Common. The few trees whose leaves had opened were slumping under rain. I went underground again, not recalling the child, barely noticing him asleep on the platform.

In Harvard Square I saw Lydia carrying her lawyer's briefcase. Thirty years ago we met here at a demonstration asking for the vote, but after a while we turned away to attend to our own lives. I thought I would forget the amputation that severed my worlds, though phantom limbs still ached.

"Are you going to vote?" I asked her.

"No. I don't live there any more, and I won't go back."

I called the man I divorced twenty years ago. "You can vote tomorrow."

"Are you sure?"

"The Consul said it's okay with both countries."

The day we became Americans the court clerk told us to remove our gloves if we were wearing them, raise our hands and pledge allegiance to the flag, foreswearing all others. I thought Pretoria a pain of the past.

His joy took me aback.

A FTER THE CIVIL WAR THAT FOLLOWED the Revolution of 1917 my father heard that the streets of

Johannesburg were paved with gold. In Vilna people talked about that golden world and about the world they knew, where Stalin did not like Jews. My father chose, promising his new bride he would send money and a ticket as soon as he could. That was 1929, the year that golden worlds crashed. It took him six years to earn her fare.

In their years apart my mother sang to her infant son about a land with raisins and almonds fit for the Messiah. She took her rosy child to the dairy and watched him drink a cup of milk. Sometimes she bought him a sugar bun and watched him eat. Years later she would quote her landlady's chiding: Why don't you eat something yourself? Watching her son was luxury enough, she said. In her telling it seemed a sunny morning. Before the War. A golden time.

At the border a custom's official noticed a book bound in soft calfskin — Pushkin, a bourgeois luxury — and confiscated her high school prize. He told her he too loved poetry and complimented her on the child gripping her hand, saying he had beautiful eyes, like hers.

The ship stopped in Ireland. Her last sight of Europe was soft as white midsummer nights. When she walked along the Liffey, men smiled at her and her son. She felt pretty and proud and whispered to him about the father they would soon see.

Waiting for her those six years in Johannesburg, he was without English and without steady work, sharing a room with two other immigrants. He had one jacket and two pairs of pants. One night he woke to see a thief climbing out of the window with the jacket he had hung over a chair.

He often saw darkness in front of his eyes. Once he went to the General Hospital and lay there with his head swathed in white. She used to say she dreamed about him that very night, his face cut and masked.

They escaped Europe's savagery just in time, and I was born where dust, thirst and lightning crack the earth and the people. Farmers burn dead grass in spring to purge each year of the one before. The scorched roots hold the blackened soil until the fields turn green with fresh blades tender as a child.

In Beit Street, where we lived in one room, I was sitting on the front steps when a boy led an ox-wagon by, loaded with watermelons. A buyer answered his call, and the sample he cut sparkled like sugar crystals. Like milk and honey, almonds and raisins. The melon and the oxen were huge, the other side of the street far away.

MY BIRTH CERTIFICATE GIVES THE NAME of the town as Doornfontein, a fountain surrounded with thorns. If the Consul faxed Pretoria, he would learn that's where I was a child. I had not expected to vote. The New England rain stopped, and I went to walk along the Charles. Cherry trees were in blossom. I wished for the pleasures of love. Towers glistened in the rinsed air on the other side of the river, and the dome of the State House was shining pretty as liberty, like the beacon it used to be. It's covered with real gold.

The mines where they open veins of gold are hot and take the men down like a child into fever. Every cell feels the press of deep gravity. All is dark except lamps and equipment, the miners' chests glistening like fish as they breathe the dust of gold and quartz until their lungs are caked with it. Their wives are far away. The children do not know their fathers. I wished I could vote for a world where children can know their parents and parents can know their children.

Five years ago they killed Stompie in scandalous circumstances. I never met him, but I heard how the little butt was stamped out. Those who killed him had learned the lessons of the country — that laws do not apply to all and any wanton wish may be acted in secret. The law accused a woman who carried herself like a queen when her husband was still in prison. To this day she claims innocence. She walked out of the courtroom defiant, holding her fist high, but her husband followed looking humbled by pain. Afterwards he said they would separate, and put her out of his life as quietly as that man could. If I voted for him, I'd have to vote for her too. The slate of candidates allowed no choice. Perhaps there is never a choice, no world where candidates are innocent and revolution heals.

THE PAVING CHANGED UNDER MY FEET. I looked down and saw the spiral pattern in the sidewalks in Lourenço Marques before it became Maputo and war destroyed its grace. Perhaps they will rebuild the Polana Hotel in my lifetime, and tourists will come again to drink vinho verde and eat prawns. I had never noticed this paving in Boston. I added the symbols of infinity underfoot to the pleasures of the city, like its blocks of slate, stretches of herringbone brickwork, cobbles and, near Winthrop Square, the Boston Bricks bronze that recalls the works of the city, its cod and spools of thread, its boots and computer chips. I rejoiced in the city's wit, its trompe l'oeil mural of a dome in cross-section and Mayor Curley seated on a bench near City Hall like a man still alive, as though mortal time had withdrawn, as it would in the day at hand, when the Election would knit my divided countries, heal hatreds and give names to people who yesterday counted less than dust.

I wished Lydia and I were still friends and walking along this river in Lourenço Marques, the spirals underfoot like medieval floor labyrinths whose true way leads through the maze to the Cross.

Something scrabbled at my legs like a dog whose owner says, "Down, down," without effect. I looked. No dog, but a boy stealing my attention while other children closed in wanting my wallet.

The boy's eyes did not yield. Two years ago a group of Gypsy children swarmed round me under a bridge in Moscow and passed quickly to my companion, Ruth, opened her money pouch and ran. I didn't know what to do or say. The children, clinging and snatching, smelled bitter, and I stood staring at their legs dry, white and flaking except at the scars.

A runner along the river saw the gang and turned toward us. A child flashed a knife, while I stood dumb, and then the children were gone. The runner, who had seen them swarming, waved and ran on, his black running suit blazoned with pink and green, all limbs, like a dragonfly big as a man. I called out, but he was gone. Ruth is still angry that I did not help her. When she sees an opportunity to harm me she will take it. As satisfaction. Many people are angry with me.

Wary of pickpockets, I turned to go back, the river now on my left, but, quick as forgetting, a wrecking crew was tearing up the way I had taken and had closed it off with red cones and yellow ribbons. I reversed again, planning to veer off as soon as I saw a street. On my left, a maze of buildings I did not recognize. I believed I could find my way if I could get my bearings. I turned to look, but the bundled body of a child blocked me, the red hood of his sweatshirt pulled over his head. Dark stuff caked his face, dirt or blood, and his legs were chapped scaly white. I couldn't tell if he was still alive. *I must tell someone,* but I stood at a loss among the spirals. I moved to feel his pulse but lost my balance and fell, cutting my hands. I saw blood and the spiral mosaic up close, chips in the dust, frost-heaved and potholed, a world of desolation. Before I could stand, leather boots passed my face, angry and ready to kick. I pulled myself up and saw people walking away. The child was gone.

It's nothing new for people to kill children.

I walked around looking but didn't see the child. Warehouses and office buildings blocked the sky and a culvert swallowed the river through a black mouth. Machinery was grinding somewhere nearby, metal scraping on metal, hissing and crushing concrete, as in a mine where they crush gold and stone and men. When the dust and litter gusted up, I shut my eyes to slits. The buildings' shadows felt cold, and seeing a glowing doorway ahead I moved toward it and the smell of bread. Men were running from the fiery oven, carrying wooden trays covered with white napkins that were plumped with loaves breathing beneath them.

My father delivered bread every day, rising when it was still dark. He came home for a cup of tea at ten and gave me a penny, and I ran to Mrs Haak's to buy green peas. She tore a quarter sheet of newspaper off its nail, twisted it into a cone and dropped in a handful of pods. I sat on the front steps and savored them seed by seed.

At the bakery's doorway I glanced at the ovens and saw a stocky man wearing round glasses, a scholar pushing trays into the fire, sweating. My young father. Our eyes met, but the men carrying loaves ran between us, and he turned back to his labor like a man who dared not stop. When the men had passed, I didn't see him. My father died worn and gray, pounded clean like cloth washed with stones.

THE GANG WHO HAD SWARMED ROUND ME before were running at the end of the alley. I turned left, seeing a way between the buildings, but they rushed forward. I saw Stompie among them. When they caught me, they pushed me past a cairn of stones and forced me through a door painted dirty aqua into the police station. The lobby was filled with a cage, and a man at a wooden counter was leaning on his elbows talking to the official on the other side. In Moscow our guide insisted we report the theft under the bridge. We waited, staring at the plumbing and wiring, and ran out of things to say. Our guide came back with a policeman who was pulling the child that scrabbled at my feet and two others, one holding onto his mother's skirt. Another mother with an infant in arms came along behind. Our guide did not want to translate when we said we refused to testify, but in the end she had nothing else to say. Even then, they did not release us until we listened to a detective explain that Moscow was troubled with criminals — Gypsies, Armenians, Georgians, Azerbaijanis. He did not say Americans, and he did not say Jews, no need.

The gang pushed me through the lobby past people working in offices, without purpose, slow and pallid. Down a shadowy corridor a toilet with its door open made sniveling sounds and smelled of ammonia. Did Stompie snivel when they beat him? They pushed me into an office where my father was facing the Consul and talking in a hoarse voice. He stopped to cough, raising his manacled hands to cover his mouth. His sleeves were rolled up, and I could see the elbows still gray and chapped. My father grew up an orphan — his parents died on the trek from the Pale when the Russians forced Jews to leave — and no one ever put oil on his skin. It remained parched through all his years of worry and chapped dark in winter.

When he saw me, he broke off. The Consul accused: The Jews are prone to crime. They are Mafia. My father would remain in prison until he confessed and gave the names of others. Gray and bald, he looked through thick glasses and broke into the cancer cough of his last months. A fuzz of white hairs covered his ear holes. The Consul told the toughs to take him away. I could not restrain myself and pulled forward to put my arms around him, weeping. But they would not let us touch. Looking at me sadly, as when we parted the last time, he let himself be led away shambling. The Consul turned to me. "Sit."

Officials were hustling a prisoner past the door, a big man who looked like the bodyguard found guilty of beating Stompie to death. The woman he used to guard was not there. She would never let them hustle her along like that. She would frighten them all with her glare. "With our matches and our necklaces," she would warn, and no one would dare silence her.

"Why do you want to vote?"

I checked the cuts on my hands and told the Consul about that night in Pretoria when I was working late and heard men's voices and a dragging sound in the open passageway the servants used, then the sigh of the lift and other groans and thumps. I switched off my light and went to the window and heard sobbing give way to screaming. Reaching the other side of the street they hit him, hit him, hit him. He was still screaming as they banged the van doors shut.

"What did you do?"

"I called the police."

"And?"

"They asked for the policemen's identity. I couldn't give it."

"And?"

"I called the newspaper."

"And?"

"They said it wasn't news." News that year was the two policemen who put hoses in the mouths of prisoners and forced them to drink until the stomach of one burst.

"And?"

"I left."

"But now you want to vote."

"I was born there. You've got my birth certificate." He made a note to investigate, and I became furious. I was ready to yell at every petty Pushkin-thief stealing books and gold fillings while complying with the law and the demands of the job. In the calm voice of an official who will not be disturbed by someone who doesn't matter, he warned, "You are copying your mother when she played victim," as though he knew every word in my mind. He called for someone to lead me away. The sergeant who came to take me had calm features and led me to a mansion whose great stairway was barred with cast iron. He was my father's driver.

O NE CAGE SAT ON THE LANDING under the Palladian window and another on the landing higher up. He opened the first cage and said, "Wait here," and closed it and left. There was still enough light for me to see my father sitting on a cot in the next cage with his elbows on his knees and his head in his hands.

He looked up and smiled. "What are you doing here, Monkeyface?"

I told him about my walk by the river. "And you, Dad. What are you doing here?"

"I'm putting my stamp collection in order. It was quite a mess."

"I also have a hard time getting papers in order."

"I've found really valuable stamps. Unique. Much better than I knew."

"So how are you setting them in order?"

"I used to do it by country and denominations. But the countries were changing names and currencies, everything, so I tried a thematic collection. You remember. Birds. Fish. Some real beauties."

"Have you seen the new stamps of Karroo flowers? Like stones that open after rain."

"Remember the Namaqualand daisies the spring you came to visit me? Such a beautiful excursion! A sea of gold."

"A long time ago."

"You know, I started my collection when I was eleven. Wait! That's it! I started with stamps on a letter from Cape Town. It's come right back to me. A penny stamp." He stood up and walked to a set of shelves set in the wall, still talking. "Jan van Riebeck's landing. A black ship and red border, perforated. Here it is! Now I'll be able to get the collection in order. That's the right beginning. I just couldn't find it."

"I don't understand."

"I'll show you later." He fell into a meditation. "Remember that story I used to tell you about the fool of Chelm who went to the bathhouse?"

"The one who tied a piece of string round his finger to remind him who he was without his clothes on?"

"That one."

"And how he lost the string, and another fool found it and had the same idea and tied it round his finger?"

"And the first fool said to the second fool, 'All right, you are me. But then who am I?'"

We both laughed. It was his favorite story. When his parents died, he wandered off the path on that journey from the Pale and got lost in the snow, and when he woke he could not remember who he was.

"Tell me another story."

"Are you a little girl again, Monkeyface?"

We talked about the penny he used to give me every morning. "You remember the time you gave me a tickey instead, and I ran to Mrs Haak's expecting three times as many peas, and she gave me the same as always? I was so disappointed."

"She must have been giving you more than a penny's worth every day," he laughed and broke out coughing and could not stop. I could not do anything about his suffering. When he recovered enough to breathe, I asked, "Will you ever be better?"

"Don't worry, I'm in good hands. Whatever happens will be what must happen." He was not going to say more about it, or where this tone of peace came from.

Just then we heard sobbing. "Don't let it worry you," he said.

"It sounds terrible."

"It's all right. We are at peace."

I heard crying like that back in Beit Street from the room where my nanny and my father's driver slept. My mother said again and again, "It's only a cat." Every day, while my father was drinking tea in the kitchen, the driver sat on the back step and drank his tea from an enamel mug and ate from a block of brown bread smeared with strawberry jam, setting it down on the enamel plate beside him.

"How could we live in one room and still afford a nanny?"

"They were poorer than us."

It was dark now. Was the yowling just a cat? "Tell me another story."

"Are you still a child? Sleep now, Monkeyface."

In the middle of the story about the tailor who killed seven at one blow, before the giants started fighting each other and the tailor escaped, I sat up. "I went to Russia, you know. A raven flew in through the window. Is the raven really our family crest?"

He went on with the tailor's story, and before his words swooned I saw that many things had been, like Mrs Haak's peas, gifts.

The hooligans had not hurt me.

SOMEONE PUT A HAND ON MY SHOULDER, and we picked our way along a road rustling with trees as the midsummer day opened to color — poppies, columbine, bluebells, apple blossom, gilded domes, cows, turned earth and, on graves near the church, forget-me-nots. My mother was walking by my side toward Pasternak's house. We passed a bonfire where a couple had set fire to garden waste and were kissing each other while flames leaped to the height of a young birch. We walked on, talking, each scarfed in our own past kisses. We passed a field of Bolshevik soldiers' graves in shade too dark for flowers, each stone like the other, none with names. We passed a house where drunk men were singing old Party songs my mother must have heard when she was young, working as a nurse in the Civil War after the Revolution. That hoax. I waited for her to speak, but she said nothing.

When Ruth and I were in the country our parents had left and we had never known, a woman we met told us the story of her father dying of grief under Stalin, her mother sent to the gulag. Vera wore the same floral dress our whole visit, and Ruth gave her chocolates, soaps and shampoos, aspirin, band-aids and the compote she herself did not want to eat. Vera said, "When we actually saw.... Though it's what we always suspected.... The President used to have hot bliny covered with white napkins chauffeured to him!" Hearing her peddle self-pity, I did not give her things. Between Ruth and me lay disagreement, and it fed her anger at me. One day a man stopped us and asked, "Why have you come to see our suffering?"

In the quiet of birdsong I turned to tell my mother that I found this countryside full of stories she had told me, but she was gone.

TOWARD THE END OF THE LANE that leads to the spring where Pasternak drew water, a woman joined me and talked about how to translate *Alice Through the Looking-Glass*. Musing on a bread-and-butterfly, we spoke about how meaning flows from one tongue to another, one time to another, one place to another. Soon we were deep in conversation like friends who pick up the threads with ease after years apart. We scrambled down a bank where other people had come with bottles and buckets. She filled a bottle and handed it to me, and I drank, and she filled it again.

"I'll walk you home," she said. At the river she looked at my hands and said, "Dogs will smell your blood and bark."

Hooligans at the culvert threw back their heads and laughed. She grew grim. "It's impossible to get rid of them."

The river was blocked by debris. On the left it was smooth as a millpond. Not a muscle betrayed its race to the spillway. A petal was gliding to the weir. On the other side a white tumble frothed round rocks and tree roots. As we came near, blood spread in the water like smoke unfurling behind the newly killed. At the mill-dam their bodies jammed, and the froth ran pink and red. There was no mistaking the smell. I saw Stompie standing nearby, short as the stump of a felled tree. My friend took my hand. "Close your eyes." I trod where she led, finding a footing on sodden flesh. I saw my life through judgmental eyes. Ruth's. Lydia's. What I have failed to do. What I have done. My body was shaking like a puppet.

"You will leave these things behind," she said.

Stompie was at my side, holding me by my clothes to keep me steady. He took my free hand and told me about a classmate who testified as an anonymous witness. The sixth time they detained her, she said, they whipped her. Five big men stood and laughed as a smaller man swung the sjambok. In the morning they let her go. Stompie's voice cracked. She was seventeen, my age when I was so much in love with Pierre. We stood on the crest of Nugget Hill and looked over the valley where my parents lived, on streets paved with gold, where I first heard of the tailor who killed seven at one blow and got giants to fight each other, where my brother stood before the Ark and read words Jews still read. Looking at the golden mine dumps, I believed something was happening that I would never forget. I have never forgotten. Pierre wrote me about a lake among mountains. I believed he too looked straight to heaven like clear water.

Stompie continued his story. They came for her at midnight. By morning, when she was open, everything was pouring out, piss, tears, blood, yells, snot, groans, the names of her friends, the things they had done, blood and blood, whimpers. When she was empty, they let her go. She dragged herself home like a child who has just killed the one in her womb. Everyone who knew her watched her pulling herself along the road. Splinters of dead grass stuck into the air. Water lay milky with soap in rut pools. She came to the place where her parents lived. The corrugated iron door hung askew. Weeks passed before they took her again and held her for six weeks, and in the courtroom she said what they told her to say.

My translator friend on my left and Stompie on my right guided me along the river's curve, bringing the city and its golden dome into sight.

"It's over," Stompie said. "Now she can vote too."

"Really over? Can it be?"

I was asking about the woman he had trusted. Would voting for her forebode another hoax revolution? He lowered his eyes and closed his lips. It felt like a rebuke. Did I expect history to become clean, like a rich suburb? We walked along the river toward Harvard Yard. The setting sun caught a gate of cast iron lacing blackness to fire, and we took a shortcut through a street lined with jacarandas. They were dropping blossoms like tears, and among their branches doves were talking the patois I have never heard outside my own land. When we reached my door, they wished me well and walked away in a quiet night white as milk and pouring through times and places that used to seem separate.

A T THE STATE HOUSE STOMPIE WAS DANCING with friends. I came alone. Families had come three generations together and were taking photographs to show children and grandchildren that here on this great day, the Election, you see me with your mother, sister, aunt. An official yielding his shift told of an old man who had taken twenty minutes and came out of the booth with tears still falling. We had all been hearing about weeping. There, across the two Atlantics, so many had died. Bill. Albert. Steve. Nat. Percy. Victoria. Matthew. Stompie. Carol's sister. Mosiuoa's brother. Barney's father. Themba's brother. Others whose names are lost, like the Bolshevik soldiers'. Some broke before they died. Adrian named his friends and is still, I hear, enduring himself. And the girl in Stompie's class.

I retrieved the certificate that says I was born in Doornfontein and cast my vote. It felt like an ordinary business among bureaucrats who checked that I am who I am. ·

The Box with a Bulbous Blister of Glass

Francesc Torres

To say that Viktor Dementiev had a major influence on 20th-century Russian literature would be an understatement. He was, after all, the man responsible for the demise of avant-garde counterrevolutionaries such as Babel, Pilniak, Mandelstam and Kliuviev, plus countless other ideological sinners swallowed up and digested in the frozen entrails of the Auschwitz-without-ovens of Kolima. He was at once the instrument of destruction, the eye of absolute power and the lightning bolt of a mediocre god uncontested in a mire of fear. He managed to be all this with relatively little in his hands — just an ingenious contraption of steel plates, levers and springs, all working for the benefit of a blinking bulbous blister of glass.

From the beginning of his assignment in 1933, when he was told to trail Osip Mandelstam and photograph any meetings with Trotskyist sympathizers — or, indeed, with anyone at all, just as long as the picture was inane enough to interpret any way one wanted — he had had to work with an assortment of old and unwieldy American and German cameras. In 1938, however, because of a special case, he was given a brand new 1.2, 50 mm Zorki, a top-notch camera, the Russian carbon copy of the German Leica. Such a rip-off was not considered humiliating either to the pride of the proletariat or to its capacity to come up with a revolutionary (no pun intended) design; it was perceived as...a shortcut. Zorki in hand, Dementiev went to work for the triumph of the Bolshevik Revolution and the preservation of his own hide.

The writer Isaac Babel became his most personal case, the aftereffects of which would accompany him until the end of his life. Babel fascinated Dementiev for reasons having to do with literature, but not necessarily with the written word. Not an anticommunist like Zamiatin, for example, Babel had been a supporter of the Revolution, fought during the Civil War against the Whites and wrote *Red Cavalry*, a tale of the Cossack First Cavalry Army for which he became very famous. Gorky held him in high esteem. So did Erhenburg, who introduced him to André Malraux, Gide and others in Paris. Unfortunately, all this attention went to his head, fueling the aristocratic sense of superiority and inflated opinion of themselves all artists tend to have unless they are of proletarian extraction. Since Babel was no proletarian, he struck a snobbish pose every time he had a chance by voicing pretentious garbage about the autonomy of artistic creation over political imperatives, joking about the stultifying effects of Socialist Realism and blasting away at mediocre bureaucratic farts telling artists and writers what to do. He went so far as to say, "A literary work is a world seen through the eyes of man, and the more man is discovered in it, in all his infinite complexity, the higher the literary quality of the work. No moral or social consideration should infringe on the development and the revelation of the writer's style. If you have a vice, refine it, elevate it to the category of art; any opposition coming from the readers or society as a whole should push you towards an even more hard-headed defense of your positions." An aristocratic statement by a pompous little ass who couldn't understand that the only true work of art is a successful revolution and the construction of a new world. But this alone should not have necessitated, perhaps, his liquidation. Bulgakov and Platonov, for instance, were neutralized but not shot. No, other events had to take place in order to have what happened happen.

Dementiev was loyal to his boss Nikolai Ivanovich Ezhov, head of the People's Commissariat for Internal Affairs, or NKVD, a black angel who kept a collection of smashed bullets tagged with the names of important victims (Smirnov, Kamenev, Zinoviev...) in the drawers of his desk. This loyalty, however, was tempered by the direction of the messenger winds from the Kremlin, the factory of reality. The weather report was this: Stalin is very fond of Lavrenti Beria; Lavrenti Beria has Stalin's ear; Lavrenti Beria is becoming more powerful by the day; Lavrenti Beria wants the NKVD.

An internal logic was at work. Since Stalin was never wrong and nothing could happen without his knowledge, Beria's rise could not be accidental. There had to be good reason for it. And if these developments seemed to indicate that Dementiev's current boss was on shaky ground, the cause of Ezhov's possible demise could only be found in himself, personally, politically and ideologically. Everyone knew that Trotskyist counterrevolutionaries had been infiltrated everywhere in the circles of power; consequently, in a neatly inverted symmetry, no one knew with any certainty who was loyal to Stalin and who was not. Ezhov's zeal and ever watchful eye, which resulted in millions of arrests and hundreds of thousands of executions of enemies of the State, could very well be a smoke screen to conceal a plot against Stalin, using the Interior Security apparatus to eliminate his political opponents with manufactured charges no one could contest.

ONE MIDSUMMER DAY IN 1938, shortly after Dementiev had left the Lubianka and was walking towards the Metropole Hotel to catch a drink, a black ZIS limousine pulled up alongside him. The man sitting next to the driver got out and grabbed him by the arm. He was initially alarmed, but the other man smiled and said, "At ease. Get in the back. There is nothing to worry about." In the car he found himself confronting a balding, bespectacled man who looked like someone fed exclusively with dairy products. It was Lavrenti Beria, and he spoke with the voice of a choir boy.

What Beria told Dementiev didn't come as a total surprise, some details perhaps, but not the gist of it. Not to him. In the realm of human behavior in general, and politics in particular, if you can imagine a situation, no matter how unthinkable, it has already happened. Besides, the light cast on a particular subject always produces shadows, the sort of environment Dementiev needed in order to exist.

Ezhov was, Beria said, conspiring to assassinate Stalin; he was in touch with known Trotskyists; his wife, Evgenia Salomonova, a notorious vulvic tigress with an agenda of her own was also involved, and so was the writer Isaac Babel, one of her many lovers and a man already under suspicion for espionage and disseminating anti-Soviet propaganda during his several trips abroad.

Beria did not want the usual fare for this case. Simply writing up a run-of-the-mill, self-incriminating declaration and then terrorizing the suspect shitless until he signed was too graceless a technique to suit the case that was going to make him the new head of the NKVD. He wanted a documented work of art, a jewel of exquisite craftsmanship; above all, he wanted to amuse Stalin, give the old bastard a laugh.

The plan hinged on the dissolute sexual behavior of the main characters in the brewing ideological auto-da-fé. Presenting the enemies of the State as feeble sexual perverts would, needless to say, introduce an entertaining twist to the traditionally boring political trials. The structure of the plot read like a novel: Babel was fucking Salomonova in order to place himself in Ezhov's inner circle, while at the same time showing his *sang froid* by possesing the wife of one of the most lethal men in the Soviet Union. Dangerous, exciting and very literary. Salomonova, on the other hand, was using her bed to manufacture power, ritually sealed through the exchange of bodily fluids; she felt smarter, bolder, more daring than her very powerful husband, whom she despised. How could she be so confident she would not be found one morning floating face down in the Moscova river? Simple. Ezhov, the purifying fire of the Revolution, was a secret homosexual. She knew it. He knew that she knew, and the arrangement was therefore stable.

All these details, including Babel's exploits, were known to the Kremlin, given Stalin's interest not only in what Russian writers wrote but what they did, what they ate and whether or not they moved their bowels regularly. Stalin was fascinated by artists in general, by this strange breed of people who do utterly irrelevant things for equally irrelevant people and then, amazingly, behave as if they are life's center of gravity. He was mesmerized by their arrogance and pleased by the thought that he could, if he wanted, send them all to a labor camp for life. Or worse.

Yes, all these details were known. Now was the time to put them to use, but first they had to be turned into proof that ideological deviation is the origin of all deviations. That was the job

Beria assigned Dementiev, with the distant knowledge of God in all His possible manifestations: Molotov, Voroshilov, Kaganovich and Stalin himself.

THE MAN WITH THE SMILING FACE who had ushered Dementiev into the back seat of the black car that killed the anticipated pleasure of a drink was the deliverer of a wonder: the brand new camera produced especially for the NKVD. It even had the agency's seal engraved on the upper part of its silver casing. It had the look, weight and cold feel of a gun.

The plan was simple. Dementiev was expected to photograph the newly appointed enemies of the people with their clothes off and having a ball. He chuckled as he wondered what criteria would be used to determine what constitutes a petty-bourgeois fuck as opposed to a Bolshevik one. No doubt the dividing line between orthodoxy and heresy is a very thin one when it comes to sex, political ideology and religion, if this last were still legal. That would explain why sex is rarely practiced in public and why, in politics, what is said is always what people, especially those in power, want to hear. Truth, naked or clothed, has no place in the making of history.

In Ezhov's case there were no fine points. Homosexuality had no room in the Revolution. A clear-cut issue. He was dead meat.

Things proceeded at a brisk pace. Making the arrangements to set up shop to photograph Babel and Salomonova together was easy. They always met at her place, a large apartment in a building for important Party people, when Ezhov wasn't there. The aparatchik in the apartment above got a phone call and was sent on an extended absence, but not before he had made a big deal, as instructed, to everyone in the building about his upcoming official trip. Dementiev showed up shortly afterwards posing as a relative come to take care of the place. Taking advantage of a few occasions when Ezhov and Salomonova's apartment was empty, a peephole large enough to fit the lens of a camera was drilled in a particularly baroque spot in the ceiling directly over their bed. The flip side of this hole expanded up into a cavity large enough to accommodate Dementiev's head, hands and camera. From there he went hunting.

He didn't have to wait long for his prey, but it wouldn't have mattered because he was being thoroughly entertained. Salomonova was receiving a lot of men, all of whom she fucked. He could identify a few known faces; others were new to him, but he photographed them all anyway because he was sure that it was only a matter of time before the pictures could be of use at the Lubianka. In the final analysis, though, he simply liked watching.

Dementiev liked watching Salomonova in particular because it was obvious that she loved sex. There were in her encounters both passion and tenderness. Perhaps a woman can fake these to an innocent lover, but not to a detached observer trained to judge people by what they do, not what they say. Watching her drove him crazy. Each photographic session left him maniacally aroused, forced to seek relief in the middle of the night with any of the female informants who owed him favors. Waiting hours for something to happen was excruciatingly boring, spending hours on his belly was torture, but Dementiev did not mind the harshness because he was looking forward to the events.

And then, one day, Babel showed up. Dementiev slid silently into position long before the writer and Salomonova got into bed. "That chubby little bastard is soon going to be lying on something softer than this servant of the Party is," he thought. After a while they came in. Salomonova was already fully undressed, but Babel kept his undershirt and socks on, suspenders and all. This is how they made it and this is how they were photographed. Dementiev took special care this time, since it involved two out of the three principal conspirators, shooting a full roll of film and putting particular emphasis on the most imaginative moments of their performance.

Babel did not look like much physically, but he was a good lover, had a reputation as a womanizer and was not too discriminating; he was once heard saying, "Don't waste your time going after intellectual women. Take lovers among factory workers and peasant women, they do not pretend." At any rate, he was experienced and did things to Salomonova that Dementiev had never seen except in pre-revolutionary pornographic postcards.

*E*ZHOV WAS MORE DIFFICULT. A master at getting people in trouble, he was a master at keeping himself out of it. Beria came up with the solution in a very handsome young actor who was being coerced into becoming an informant inside Moscow's Academic Arts Theater. The Lubianka had him on a short leash because he was homosexual and told him he was heading straight for a labor camp unless he cooperated. Beria offered him a way out; he could become the bait to get Ezhov. The young fellow accepted.

He was planted at a reception at the Kremlin and made himself available; Ezhov went for him with a strange mixture of caution and determination. The two were left alone for a while to make sure Ezhov wouldn't get wind of anything amiss. The best place for Dementiev to take his pictures was going to be the theater; Ezhov frequently went there to interrupt rehearsals and force everybody to kiss his ass and listen to his ideas about theater as a political tool to educate the masses. When the time was right, he would abandon his audience with a frozen smile on their faces and roam around backstage where he would casually run into his young actor. This convoluted choreography of desire would end up in the forgotten depths of the basement, where the two of them embraced in the midst of gigantic backdrops of sunny Socialist landscapes at harvest time surging up from behind kilometers of racks of peasant costumes. Dementiev, hiding under tons of dusty mujik jackets and guarded by the towering painted figure of a young peasant girl with her armored breasts pointing toward the completion of the Five Year Plan, got his pictures.

This time he didn't get excited, but he was intrigued at the sight of a man responsible for as many deaths as a biblical plague caressing another man. He was astonished at how vulnerable in his secret, and therefore human, Ezhov seemed.

WITH THE DIRT IN HIS HANDS Beria went to work. He told Ezhov that some high-ranking military officers had become aware of a Trotskyist plot to assassinate Stalin. They had names, among them those of his wife, her former husbands and some of her lovers, of whom the most notorious was Isaac Babel. At this point some pictures of Salomonova were shown to drive the point home. Beria delivered the *coup de grâce* when he told Ezhov that claiming ignorance on the subject would only mean that he was involved in the plot himself or else that he was pathetically incompetent, since he didn't know what was going on in his own bedroom. Incompetence was as despicable as treason, since he was married to a woman who wanted to kill Stalin. Granted, the Army was being investigated and purged of Zinovievist reactionaries, so there was a possibility that he was being implicated in a counterrevolutionary attempt to behead the NKVD. The photographs, on the other hand, were no invention. To make a long story short, Ezhov was put in the desperate position of having to show that his nose was clean.

Up to now Ezhov couldn't have cared less about his wife's sexual adventures; he had needed her as a cover for his own. That her infidelities had become known, however, was mortifying for a power-hungry gnome like him. The additional fact that she could be used to destroy him, whether the political charges against her were true or not, was unbearable and to be avoided at all costs. Ezhov didn't hesitate. He immediately opened an investigation into his own wife and scores of people in her entourage.

To be investigated in Russia in the late 30s was tantamount to being found guilty, and Salomonova lost her position as editor of *USSR in Construction* and *Illustrated Daily*, and everybody avoided her to save their own skin. She wrote desperate letters to a husband who had become the instrument of her annihilation: "Nikolai! I implore you.... I insist that a fair examination of my entire life be done.... I cannot come to terms with the idea of being accused of duplicity and crimes that I did not commit...."

In October 1938 Evgenia Salomonova, in the middle of her debacle, entered a sanitarium near Moscow in a state of deep depression. A month later she died of poisoning by Luminal.

On December 7, 1938, Ezhov was replaced by Lavrenti Beria as the head of the NKVD. He was left on his own for a while, like a fly banging hopelessly against a window pane, before being arrested four months later. He was charged with treason, counterrevolutionary conspiracy, plotting to assassinate Stalin and scores of consummated assassinations, including that of his own wife. He was also treated to a collection of photographs of himself having sex with another man in the bowels of a theater. His interrogation went on for months, in the course of which he implicated dozens of people — one of whom was Babel. Ezhov was found guilty, shot in the back of the head in early 1940 and airbrushed out of all official photographs. This was the end of the period of terror known as the *ezovschina*.

The photograph of Isaac Babel at the Lubianka after his arrest on May 16, 1939, the last ever taken of him, marked the beginning of a long ordeal. The author penned his own interrogation for the benefit of his lazy inquisitors. His last literary work is preserved in the KGB headquarters to this day. "Make sure our daughter does not grow up to be unhappy," were his last words to his wife before he was taken away. Babel was shot on January 27, 1940, only a few days after Ezhov. The ashes of the writer and the black angel are mixed together in Common Grave Number 1, Inhumation of Unclaimed Remains from 1930 to 1942, Donskoi cemetery, only a few yards from Evgenia Salomonova's grave, the three of them reunited under the skin of a planet concerned only about its own revolutions around the sun.

VIKTOR DEMENTIEV MANAGED TO SURVIVE the purges, the war, Stalin himself. Retired with a pension, he managed even to survive Communism, the eschatological builder of concentration camps in its search for the Garden of Eden. He died in his chair in 1994, on the same day that Yeltsin's tanks were bombarding, in the name of democracy, the seat of the legally elected Russian Parliament. On the floor, just beneath his dangling hand, they found a few pornographic pictures from the 30s showing a chubby man in his undershirt, his socks held up by suspenders and his face buried deep between the legs of a woman who didn't seem to be faking her pleasure.   V

The Fire Circle

Scott L. Malcomson

THE MOST IMMEDIATELY ALARMING THING was how easy I found preaching to be. That morning in Elohim City we all had on our Sunday best, 80 or so worshippers, eager for the week's highlight; we had tiptoed through the mud of the compound to keep our shoes looking respectable. Only one man wore fatigues — James Ellison, noted ex-terrorist, convicted racketeer and far-right Christian militant, accompanied by his most recent, young and evidently pregnant wife, Angie, who wore a full-cut yet light dress. A few men carried sidearms, knives or semi-automatic rifles of the sort that, with a little tinkering, can be altered to fully automatic. The rest of us, in shirts and ties, in modest cotton dresses with some polyester for durability — at least in a clean shirt and unwrinkled slacks — we were as unarmed as on the day we were born.

The primary purpose of this tiny community, according to its residents, is to worship God, known as Yahweh (pronounced ya-hoo-wuh) or the Father, under the loose, avuncular guidance of Reverend Robert Millar, known to all as Grandpa, who set up camp here with a few followers in 1972. He wanted to call his settlement Councillor but somewhere else in Oklahoma already had that name so he chose Elohim City, City of Gods (the Hebrew plural). A secondary purpose of Elohim City is to guard in isolation a group of white Christians. According to local interpretation of Scripture, white people, not Jews, are the true Israelites, Yahweh's chosen. As Israelites they bear a responsibility to gird themselves for the years of Tribulation announced in Revelation. The Tribulation in America is expected to take the form of a race war, following which those Israelites who remain will lead the way in building the Kingdom of Righteousness.

I had not expected to preach, and I had never composed a sermon in my life, but Reverend Millar, knowing that I am the son and grandson of Baptist ministers, asked me to address his flock. This was how the reverend and I got along with and understood each other — as members (me rather by proxy) of the fraternity of those who deliver the Word. For me, in this American Protestant lower-class world, to have refused to speak would have been *ungracious*, therefore impossible. But what could I say to a congregation, however small, of lightly armed white-separatist Christian fundamentalists waiting in serene, perhaps hungry anticipation of global travail and horror in a remote mountaintop commune in Oklahoma? What could I say that would neither encourage nor offend? I considered these questions as three teenagers made their way through a tinkling tune called "Fighting the Beast." Owing to the peculiarity of their beliefs, the worshippers at Elohim City have, for the most part, to write their own songs. As the singing wound down, I thought of what I had seen my father do numberless times. First, smile. This is a small audience, so make brief eye contact with three or four people and keep hand gestures gentle. Humbly thank the local pastor, who has just given you an overly kind introduction. Say something funny. Play with the microphone for a second; appear strong yet slightly awkward, slightly confused. Let the audience know that you need their help and protection; give them that opportunity. But let them know, too, that you can bear the load. Then start telling stories. Writers and preachers alike have faith in the power of stories.

> As our happiness goes
> With the terror,
> The puddles left by the rain,
> As the blood shed of the victims,
> The cold makes us shiver,
> As does the terror,
> It is unwanted,
> Yet it comes.

So wrote Amy McDonald, of the 7th grade, in her poem "Terror," published in a volume intended to commemorate the 1995 bombing of the Alfred P. Murrah Federal Building in Oklahoma City. Most of the poems were by adults and ended with evocations of the unity of America, God's nation, and of how everything, even this millenarian's charnel house, was part of His plan. There was much mention of angels and how the murdered little children had gone "home." The poems actually written by children, however, lacked such reassurances. Sixth-grader Joe Sanders, for example, ended his poem with, "I'm told it happened by one/ Terrorist's hand,/ As long as I live,/ I will not understand."

After the last of the dead were found and the remains of the building carted away, a rickety Cyclone fence was erected around the site. Even months after the bombing, the building's former parking lot still had bits of jetsam, including one damaged office chair, bravely upright on its casters. The walls of boarded-up buildings overlooking the lot bore graffiti: a bold tirade argued that God demands justice; a smaller statement read, "We Should Have Looted." At the center of the parking lot survives a tree. In another culture, perhaps, that tree would have become a shrine and been known as, say, the Tree of Hope. But here, the fence itself was a shrine. Christmas trees were bound to it, as were pine boughs that formed crosses, holiday cards, T-shirts left by visitors, business cards, flowers, stuffed animals, a child's pair of red sneakers, a message from two Brooklyn visitors ("God Bless America and Help US ALL") and a photo of a now-dead child, put there by "Mom and Dad," with the legend, "Happy Birthday Blake Kennedy."

The Oklahoma City bombing was a family affair. Everywhere hung pictures of angels and references to them, reflecting the belief that dead children, being by definition innocent, immediately become angels. Most of the images showed white children and white angels, even though a great many of the dead in Oklahoma City were not white. The other striking feature of the shrine was its crosses, made from two sticks wedged into the fencing. Dozens of these primitive relics covered the fence, where, in contrast to the stuffed animals and the streaked, sagging T-shirts, they survived unharmed by the weather. A small but regular host of visitors drove by the fence of relics or walked along it, pausing to read messages. Beneath the luffing T-shirts and the angels, a russet murk of mud and water flowed from the building site, soiling the shoes of pilgrims.

The Heartland Chapel stood cattycorner and down a few steps from the old parking lot, a simple, sturdy wooden structure, quickly built, with a clutch of pews. A brusque wooden cross had been planted in a plinth made from fragments of the burned building. Toy animals lay piled higgledy-piggledy at its base. One would think no adults had died. Leaning against the plinth was a presentation in plastic laminate bordered with pennies (for weight). Within the plastic sheets someone had placed a postcard. On one side was a photo of two little boys, Chase and Colton Smith, playing; on the other was a passage in a typeface made to look like handwriting: "While our worlds have been forever changed and we no longer suffer, our family grieves deeply. Please continue to pray for them." It took me a moment to realize that the family had given these words to their dead children in order to request a prayer for themselves.

The term "heartland" indicates Oklahomans' belief that their state is the most pure example of America. Some evidence suggests that this faith also preys on the minds of the sort of people who blow up buildings. James Ellison, for example, of Elohim City, discussed with his comrade, the late Richard Wayne Snell, whether they ought to fire a rocket at the Murrah building back in 1983. Part of their thinking was that no one would expect such an attack in the heartland — and they were right. Oklahomans' faith in the purity of their Americanness and their Christian goodness was shaken by the murder of 168 people downtown in their capital city; they seem to have reacted, for the most part, by clinging to that faith more tightly.

IN THE MONTHS AFTER THE APRIL 19 BOMBING, according to one federal agency, thefts of explosives and other materials used by the Oklahoma City bombers rose dramatically. A train in Arizona was derailed and credit claimed by a right-wing group; two military boys, admirers of the Ku Klux Klan, murdered a black couple; in Arkansas, a bomb went off with, near it, a note alluding to the federal government's "conspiracy" against its people. Incidents occur here and there, the only consistency so far being that they have all taken place in one heartland or another.

Oklahoma remains something of a center for domestic terrorism. Here are some excerpts from a transcript of an FBI surveillance tape made seven months after the Oklahoma City bombing. The recorded meeting took place in and around a decaying, one-story, white wood-framed house in rural Vernon, Oklahoma, which had been turned into the Universal Church of God (Yahweh) by Reverend Willie Ray Lampley, known as Ray. The church was set up like a home office, with printing devices, desks, wall calendars with scrawled deadlines, stacks of pamphlets and, next to the front door, a framed photograph of the Branch Davidian compound in Waco, Texas, burning. Apart from this photograph, there were no devotional items in Reverend Lampley's church, no altars, no chalices or crosses. Along with his church, Lampley also had a tiny militia. The speakers are Lampley, 65; his wife, Cecilia, 47; Richard Schrum, the FBI informer, wired for sound; and J.D. Baird, 53, a churchmember. (U) indicates unintelligible. "C four" is an explosive made from cooking down ammonium nitrate fertilizer, the same explosive used in Oklahoma City. The official transcriber tries to reproduce speech; "thank," for example, usually means "think."

> **LAMPLEY:** And, now, we fill that to about like that with black powder, so that this is directly in contact with it and it'll flame.
>
> **SCHRUM:** Uh, huh.
>
> **LAMPLEY:** We'll fill the rest of that, with this. Crimp it good, and then put these wires out like, well we n...we'll need to put the wires out this way. So what we'll do is we'll wrap this with a *(buzzing noise)* 'lectrical tape and then wrap those wires back this way so that all the shock goes directly into the C four. *(Squeak)*
>
> **SCHRUM:** Uh, huh.
>
> **LAMPLEY:** So that's what's on the mind.

....

(They discuss grinding explosive powder in a kitchen blender.)

SCHRUM: You thank that'll do it, I mean I don't know that much about a blender.

LAMPLEY: We make flour, with our blender.

SCHRUM: Oh you do?

....

LAMPLEY: Yeah. Corn and make meal out of it.

SCHRUM: Oh you do?

LAMPLEY: Yeah.

SCHRUM: I'll be doggone.

LAMPLEY: We're survivors.

The next day, federal agents entered the church and several trailer homes around it and seized, among other items, guns, a toaster (allegedly used to provide a detonator), a blender from Sears, six bags of C-4 and *The Anarchist's Cookbook*. Reverend Lampley was arrested in a McDonald's parking lot on the turnpike. He, his wife and J.D. Baird were jailed in Muskogee. Richard Schrum soon went into hiding. "I really don't feel good about Ray being in jail, because he was like a friend," Schrum told the Muskogee *Phoenix*. "I really cared about the guy. I feel like Judas."

I first saw Reverend Willie Ray and Cecilia Lampley and J.D. Baird in a Muskogee courtroom during a hearing. They entered in chains. Ray was bent over, his face pale and blotchy, the sleeve of a long undershirt dangling, ripped, from beneath his dark green prison jumpsuit. Baird was no more formidable, though the transcript revealed him to be in training for combat. When he briefly took the stand and was asked to recall a number, he reached out his hands and did the sums with his fingers. Cecilia was the youngest and healthiest of the three, her nicely coiffed brown hair just beginning to gray; she seemed almost light-hearted, following the proceedings with care, chatting animatedly with Ray and their attorneys at the defense table.

I next saw Reverend Lampley in prison. We sat in separate rooms and spoke by telephone. We had to lean forward to see each other through a small window, squinting because the glass was murky.

Reverend Lampley believed that the UN, "the Beast of Revelations 13," was set to invade the United States. Why the United States? Because "the American people are from the tribe of Ephraim, from the House of Joseph, we're Israelites." The Antichrist is coming to punish us, the true Israelites, because we have been in rebellion against God's law. Through his church, Reverend Lampley had tried for the past seven years "to warn the [American] people either to get in harmony with God's law or the whole system is coming down. So that was basically the purpose of it [his ministry]....It's still the matter that, it either gets in harmony with God — well, it's too late now...."

Reverend Lampley believes he is one of the two "witnesses" mentioned in Revelation 11. What does that mean? "It simply means that, well, what we have done is we have filed lawsuits in eleven states, in federal district courts, letting them know that this conspiracy to overthrow the government of God and the government..., they have made a determination to overthrow God in the land, and this is nothing but a conspiracy and this is about to come to an end. So basically what I'm saying is, we have filed lawsuits throughout the land to *warn* everyone in political office that you either change, or you are going to die. And that's what it amounts to.

"That doesn't mean that *we're* going to kill them, it simply means that, that they are going to be *killed*. I mean, all of these officials are going to die because they refuse to obey God. It's not that it matters that they refuse to obey *me*. But they're, you know, they're going to be held *accountable.*

"Now, when this time comes — see, you notice that in that Revelations 11 it says, 'I will give power to my two witnesses'? Okay, when this power comes, and it will come, *then* these witnesses will be calling down plagues upon this nation."

AFTER THE LAMPLEYS AND BAIRD WERE ARRESTED, Reverend Robert Millar and his son John, said by the reverend to be his community's "ramrod," came to the arraignment. Reverend Lampley told the judge that Jesus Christ would serve as his defense attorney. Reverend Millar gave Reverend Lampley the thumbs-up. According to the FBI transcript, Lampley and his brethren had thought to test their bomb at Elohim City, probably owing to its isolation — six and a half miles up a rough dirt road from a lonely highway. J.D. Baird had misgivings because, as he said, "the Feds were all over that place…tryin' ta spook 'em into doin' somethin' so they can jump on their shit." This was broadly true, and Reverend Millar speaks with pride of how, during one visit, the Feds were compelled into politeness by his boys, who trained their semi-automatic weapons on them from the trees. The Feds were particularly interested in Elohim City after the April bombing because records showed two calls having been made to the compound from Timothy McVeigh's phone, one only minutes after he rented a Ryder truck. "I think he probably met some of our young lads at some gun show," Millar says, "and got our name by that means. You know, there's a certain camaraderie some people have at gun shows."

Reverends Lampley and Millar share a theology called Christian Identity, one of many religious imports we have received from Britain. It has its roots in the early and middle 19th century, when "Anglo-Israel" thought got off the ground with its leading idea that the English were among the Chosen — that they could be "identified" as Israelites. Researchers traced the royal family back to the Old Testament.

Some among the better classes of New England adopted this notion, which would reappear almost randomly until being taken up between the wars by some formidable anti-Semites, including the alcoholic newsman William Cameron, an adviser to Henry Ford during the industrialist's openly anti-Semitic period, and Gerald L.K. Smith, an influential polemicist and advocate of Christian Nationalism who believed that Jews were "sons of Satan." Christian Nationalism, according to one of its theorists speaking at a university in 1949, believed "in *racial purity, the superiority of the white race, that the white race is the bearer and protector of civilization, segregation of the races,* that *the danger to the white race comes from the aspiration of the Jewish race to dominate the world.*"

The leading architect of segregation in Oklahoma, William H. Murray, promoted Christian Identity beliefs. He ran the Constitutional Convention prior to statehood in 1907, and later served as governor (as did his son). Murray was a politician of the "colorful," Huey Long variety. Thus his nicknames, Alfalfa Bill and the Sage of Tishomingo. He had been just another tobacco roader up from Texas until he married a Chickasaw Indian from a good family — he believed the Chickasaws were also Israelites — and entered politics. He remains the most famous of the state's politicians, and is remembered affectionately in its conventional histories. They do not normally quote from his Identity-influenced 1951 book *Adam and Cain* ("Communism in the World will never be checked until the papers are free to attack the Jew as a people"), which includes a short version of "The Protocols of the Elders of Zion," nor from his 1948 volume, *The Negro's Place in the Call of Race.*

After World War II, Christian Identity thought lay somewhat

fallow, only to be adopted enthusiastically by the extreme right in the 1980s, influencing such celebrated religio-terrorist groups as Aryan Nations and the Order. These organizations committed sundry murders and bank robberies until the federal government closed many of them down. The surviving leaders then decided, in a typically semi-organized way, to promote "militias." Militias have been around in various forms for years; the direct ancestors of today's militias are the Minutemen of the 1960s. Reverend Millar told me he would be willing to serve as the "spiritual leader" of the "militia movement." He sees this as part of his calling, and the militias as leading players in the coming battles of the End Times.

REVEREND MILLAR WAS JUST FINISHING LUNCH when I knocked on his trailer door. He helped his ailing wife back to the darkened living room and onto the couch; wordless, she nearly disappeared into it. She must have been quite strong once. She has raised five children and spent two and a half decades with her husband building Elohim City up from nothing. A girl arrived to look after Mrs Millar, known to all as Grandma just as the reverend is Grandpa. Before we sat down to chat Reverend Millar cleared the dishes, adding them to the pile in the sink. The compound's water system was blocked; some of the men were out trying to fix it. His wife's health was failing, but Millar himself, at 70, was in fine shape. With a belly for ballast, a white beard and emphatic eyebrows, he appeared somewhere between Santa Claus and Joseph Smith, like an Old Testament prophet only smaller and livelier. As we spoke, he would get up often to change chairs for no apparent reason other than jumpiness: Isaiah as sprite.

Millar has made some progress in establishing himself as a spiritual leader. So many of the far-right personalities, themes, fears and hopeful plans of the last fifteen years come together in this lonely compound. On the day of the Oklahoma City bombing (and the anniversary of the Waco fire), Reverend Millar, in his clerical capacity, visited Richard Wayne Snell on death row. Snell was awaiting execution for murdering a black Arkansas state trooper in 1984. Snell had previously murdered a Texarkana pawnbroker; supposedly he had believed, wrongly, that the pawnbroker was Jewish. By the time Millar arrived, Snell had already watched the explosion on TV. Millar had visited Snell weekly during his ten years in prison and had seen much progress in the convicted man's spiritual outlook. "He deplored the loss of life same as you and I do," Millar says. According to press accounts, Snell said, at his execution, "Hell has victory," and some took this as a reference to the bombing. Reverend Millar maintains Snell's words were, in fact, "Hail His victory" — the press version was "a definite misquote." Millar took Snell's body back to Elohim City for burial.

Snell's old comrade James Ellison moved to Elohim City after serving a ten-year sentence for racketeering and married Reverend Millar's granddaughter Angie. Ellison had once had his own compound — Zarephath-Horeb, in Arkansas, about a hundred miles east of the Oklahoma border — and his own movement, The Covenant, The Sword, and The Arm of The Lord, or CSA. The compound's most famous feature, Silhouette City, was a mock American inner city, used as a practice ground for urban warfare. Ellison's followers helped pay the mortgage by robbing stores ("plundering the Egyptians"). Ellison, in the Christian Identity tradition, gradually came to understand that he was descended from King David. Reverend Millar recognized the value of his ministry by anointing him "James of the Ozarks." Federal agents surrounded Zarephath-Horeb in 1985, and Millar was brought in to convince Ellison to surrender, which he did.

Most recently, the defense attorneys for Timothy McVeigh tried to identify an international conspiracy behind the Oklahoma City bombing, a cabal of which their client could only have been the merest tool. Their investigations, and those of other interested parties, kept leading to one Andreas Strassmeir, known at Elohim City as Andy the German, who fled to Berlin; to Michael Brescia, Andy the German's roommate at Elohim City, who went underground; and to Reverend Millar.

At the kitchen table, Millar gestured toward a letter from a posse comitatus group, one more of the seemingly numberless far-right outfits that have popped up over the past fifteen years. Such groups, Millar said, look to him for spiritual guidance, and he, in turn, looks to them for a way to expand his ministry. In 1959, still just in his mid-30s, Millar suffered a heart attack. This left him with time to think and browse ("I've always been a browser"), especially in the Bible, where he noticed that the original texts had a number of names for man. "Pursuing that, I came to the conclusion that all erect bipeds are not the offspring of Adam, according to the Scripture....That led me in to a conviction that all flesh are not the same flesh."

Browsing further, Millar concluded that God "has especially chosen some people, that is, some race of people." This conclusion itself, of course, was not new. What made the interpretation fresh, to Millar, was his belief that these chosen people need "to be clearly differentiated from the, what are today called, or in the Bible are called, Jews." He maintains that northern Europeans, "these people which together compromise [sic] less than nine percent of the world population, that these people, together, are the inheritors of the promise made to Abraham, Isaac and Jacob, and that they are the lineal descendants." His is a hard multiculturalism. Cultures are, Millar believes, in part "a result of the DNA code," and not to be trifled with: "I think the destruction of any ethnic group is really a violation of respect for fellow man and of respect for God's creation." A Canadian by birth — he grew up in Kitchener, Ontario, not far from Toronto — Millar gives the Inuit as an example: modern technology has led them away from their traditions. "To impose our changes unilaterally on other cultures can be very disruptive, and also no doubt a result of a profound arrogance on our part."

Wouldn't this, I suggested, mean that he and I, both primarily, or at least patrilineally, of Scottish origin, ought to be wearing kilts, tossing cabers and so on? The answer was no, because modern technology is a white achievement and therefore part of our native tradition — even when it's brand new. "All of life is progressive and changing, and this is especially true of Caucasian man. He tends toward change and progress." We Caucasians have been inclined, "since the 1400s," toward "technological development."

"The message of Christian Identity," he said, "is the message of responsibility and obligation," that is, the responsibility of white people, as the DNA-enabled lineal descendants of Abraham, to lead. Millar phrased this within the Christian language of "stewardship," saying, for example, that under the British Empire, and often under the direction of Scottish adminis-trators, the "natives" were much better off. The expulsion of colonial administrators "has been to the disadvantage of the indigenous populations."

A spiritually successful society needs to divide tasks according to the particular geniuses of its constituent cultures. Each culture must know itself. "I think Alex Haley," Millar said, "I think he did an awful lot for white people with his book called *Roots*." One day a boy of Irish descent, a boy searching for meaning, vis-ited Elohim City. He told Reverend Millar that he was in love with a Laotian girl and asked whether he ought to marry her. Millar advised against it, because such a union would have destroyed centuries of "her beautiful culture," taken her from it, just as it would have destroyed the boy's own Irish heritage. The boy agreed not to marry her. "So that's part of what Christian Identity is."

Racial mixing is among the social developments leading us to Apocalypse. "I think we're going to have bloodshed here in America," he said. "I think we're gonna have race wars. I think we're gonna have international intervention, that is, foreign nations on our soil. And I anticipate it more shortly than in the distant future." The signs are everywhere; everything is a sign. "I think that we are scheduled for a housecleaning. That's already going on." He slowly lists the banes that are being visited upon the world as retribution against white people for having betrayed their covenant. "Earthquakes, floods, famines, pestilence, plagues. Because we've had so much, and been such terrible stewards. But I do believe that a remnant of this group is destined to be a light, an example, to the other civilizations. Following the cleansing."

DURING OUR CONVERSATION Reverend Millar changed seats several times and the girl looking after Grandma wandered into the kitchen, stared at the dirty dishes, then wandered back to the dark living room. Millar suggested we go for a walk through the compound. He was restless, and worried that our conversation might be disturbing his wife.

Why did he start Elohim City? "We felt it was what our Father wanted us to do." And how did he know? "That kind of a statement defies rational explanation." We walked along a path in the chill mountain air, and Reverend Millar jumped onto a low railing, balanced himself along its length and hopped off without even breaking his conversation. He said he had never been more content than with his present ministry. "I have this concept — and this has to do with Christian Identity emphasis, I suppose — I have this concept that the prayer, 'Thy kingdom come, Thy will be done, on earth as it is in heaven,' now that is not only a possible fulfillment, it actually will be fulfilled, His kingdom will come on earth. And then the question arises, Why should we not move in that direction?"

As we wandered along up the mountain, I mentioned to Reverend Millar Oklahoma's vivid history of racial separatism. Oklahoma history stands as a parable of the urge toward racial purity, and of that urge's pure impossibility. The Indians were first, arriving here in large numbers as a result of federal resettlement policies (to use no harsher word), most famously the Cherokees, whose Trail of Tears ended here. With the reinstitution of white supremacy following Reconstruction, blacks migrated up from the South, though a considerable population of blacks had previously arrived as slaves of the relocated Indians. One can only imagine what a Trail of Tears it was for them. In the first decade of this century, blacks organized to make Indian Territory — at the time, the eastern half of today's Oklahoma — an all-black state of the union. Their efforts failed. In 1906 various Indians held a constitutional convention to make it an all-Indian state, to be called Sequoyah. That effort also failed. Then a third effort, dominated by whites, petitioned Washington for statehood. This succeeded, and Oklahoma became a state in 1907. By 1912 racial segregation was well under way, despite immediate opposition from black activists, and Oklahoma remained a Jim Crow state until 1965. It is famous in Jim Crow lore for being the first state to segregate telephone booths.

Reverend Millar seemed to follow all this with interest. We stopped for breath, and he gestured out over his land, which stretches to the Arkansas border: "All this land that you can see there, top of that ridge and down and over, that's our land and it's paid for." This land has wild turkey, possum, raccoons, the odd mountain lion, some bear, plenty of deer. Millar's sons and grandsons are keen hunters, and "they're all crack shots," he said with pride. "This land in here, I thought nobody had ever been here for centuries," he said. "But after I was here for a number of years, I found out that there had been white men living right in these hills. How they lived, I don't know. Just the south part of our property there was a sawmill run by steam, and a whiskey still and a dozen houses. Then when it became Indian territory the white man was chased out of here and had to give his property and his buildings. And then, that was reversed again in 1907. It was white land before it was Indian territory. And then it was...." Millar paused. He is not the most educated of men, but he is clever and thoughtful and careful. "I'm as opposed to forced segregation as I am to forced integration."

I had a number of thoughts which I decided to keep to myself. It seemed that Reverend Millar and others at Elohim City were taking me at face value, so to speak. My clerical ancestry was a useful calling card; I did not mention my nearly complete absence from church over the past twenty years. In appearance, I could hardly be more Caucasian. That was useful, too, here as in so many places. Yet I also knew — it was very much on my mind in those mountains — that I had family not a hundred miles away, cousins by marriage who were part Cherokee. Their ancestors had intermarried with whites back in the old Indian lands; more white than Cherokee, these relatives had come here over the Trail of Tears, bringing their black slaves with them. (They fought on the Southern side, as did many, though not all, of the Cherokees.) I knew that, here in Indian Territory, before the Civil War, there had been some slaves of the Creeks who shared one of my family names, Lacy, which is not a common name. What would happen to their descendants in the Tribulation? I even knew that some of my distant cousins had first brought organized Christianity to these hills, which, that afternoon, made me feel faintly ashamed. There is a monument to their efforts, a short drive from Elohim City. I knew all this but kept it to myself because I wanted to "get the story," as journalists say, and because I was afraid. It seemed prudent and useful simply to be white. It usually is.

How, I asked, do Indians fit into the Christian Identity scheme? Millar said we, or rather, "we," should not force them to live "the white man's way. Let them progress on their own." But, he added, "don't force me to have one living beside me."

REVEREND MILLAR TOOK ME TO VISIT JEDDA, who lived by herself in a neat and spacious trailer. At 74, she was his eldest follower. She was as nice as could be, quiet and proper, the very figure of a good Christian woman. Reverend Millar informed her that she and I had something in common — we were both raised as Baptists. This is essential data among Protestants. In a roomful of Protestant strangers, you inquire after denominations in order to find a common language.

When Jedda was still a Baptist, she met Reverend and Mrs Millar. The Millars were doing house meetings in Florida. They would arrive in a town and work up contacts; whomever they succeeded in impressing would make a house available and spread the word that a new preacher was in town. There is a sort of non-denominational underground that exists across America, linked by the movements of itinerant preachers. They arrive one day and hold house meetings or, often, guest-preach at churches. If you are dissatisfied, if you are looking for something more than your usual church provides, you go to house meetings. Jedda was at a difficult point in her life and the Baptist church was letting her down. She was looking for something more.

Millar gave her that something. "There's a deeper spiritual experience," she said with a gracious smile. "Back to the Baptists again, the Baptist doesn't teach, and doesn't really believe, in the baptism of the Holy Spirit. And it is *real*, I have found out." I asked for specifics, but Jedda was at a loss and fluttered her hands girlishly toward Millar. He leaned forward in his easy chair and talked at length about Pentecostals and Nazarenes and Billy Graham and the varieties of Protestant experience: being saved, then sanctified, then filled with the holy spirit; the release from guilt, the awareness of being a child of God, speaking in tongues.

I watched Jedda and saw the pleasure she took in Millar's discourse on Protestant arcana. She nodded and murmured support. She seemed to respond more to sounds than to his various points of argument. He spoke in a raspy whisper, as if delivering secrets dearly bought, and littered his speech with talismans — saved, grace, Holy Spirit, sanctity. "We do not *disparage* any of those works of *grace*," he said. God "keeps coming to us. And we think that there is no limitation."

Jedda had been listening to this for some two decades, and she didn't look tired of it, not at all. Neither did Millar. "Most groups," he said, "seek to have a balance between the horizontal progress and the vertical progress, that is, reaching into the heights and depths of God, and reaching out to expand and you get a bigger church. Most try to get a balance. But I think that time will show that the vertical development, that is, reaching into the heights and depths of God, probably will take priority over the horizontal expression."

This mystical ambition "affects our relationship with our fellow man, obviously. It affects our reaction to things that government agencies do against us." I said that I didn't quite see the connection. Millar's voice took on urgency. The Bureau of Alcohol, Tobacco and Firearms, the FBI and other agencies were persecuting his church; they "manufacture preposterous stories and turn 'em, drop little tidbits, especially on TV." I still didn't see the connection. Jedda and Millar did. In their opinion, the BATF is trying to undermine God. That's the connection.

ONE MORNING, ED TOOK ME TO SEE Richard Wayne Snell's grave. I was staying with Ed and his wife, Mary Ruth, in a trailer across from Elohim City's church. (About half the houses there were trailers.) Mary Ruth is Richard Snell's daughter. I never asked her about her father because that would have been ungracious. Once, though, she and I were discussing religion, and she recalled that her father often preached, and that he was a good preacher, too.

The cemetery lies on a muddy track just beyond the burnt ground of Elohim City's fire circle, where revivals are held in summer. Three people have died here so far, two from natural causes, so there are three simple crosses now on the hillside, overlooking the fire circle. Taking care of the cemetery is one among Ed's many jobs. He showed me a rectangular depression at the head of Snell's grave; Ed plans to pour permanent concrete markers for the three dead.

From the cemetery you can look back over Elohim City, the houses and trailers scattered in no apparent order among deciduous trees and some pines. In the distance, on the left, is a pasture for the community's sheep; above and slightly to the right, the community's sawmill; and above that the mountaintop, the highest point for miles around in this stretch of the Ozarks. Everywhere the smell of woodsmoke, the gray or blue or black smoke from the dozen hearths of a dozen families in hiding.

Ed and Mary Ruth came here, he said, to get away from "the niggers" in the city, whom they feared in part because of Mary Ruth's parentage. We stood for a while on the road and Ed told me about his conversion. He had not been living right. He did this and that as a laborer, he partied with the proud drunk violence of tobacco road, he passed some time in prison. Then one day his body began to rebel. He lost his will. He was overcome with terror. He became feverish and stayed in a fever for many hours. He was being visited by an awesome power he is helpless to describe. Mary Ruth asked him if he needed a doctor, but he wanted nothing save to remain in that fever until it ended of itself.

Now, he said, people ask him, Where is the old Ed? And he replies, I don't know. I haven't seen him. He was here but now he's gone and no one knows where he went nor how to find him.

That night at Ed and Mary Ruth's trailer I sat on the porch for a while talking with Ed's friend Pete about white identity. Pete was doing his best to look like a woodsman. He'd grown a beard, kept his clothes sloppy and carried a gun. I was impressed by his appearance because it seemed a little silly. America has not been a rural country for a long time. It is urban and suburban, with a good number of small towns. Just about everyone can read and write and has electricity, running water, phones, a television, a car and relations scattered around the country. And just about no one knows how to lay up salt meat, skin a rabbit, timber a mine shaft or smoke a ham. Yet many Americans do behave as if driving a pickup (with Japanese parts) to a mall (built well after the Carter administration) is somehow akin to riding old Jessie down the road to a barn dance. Since the 1970s many Americans have adopted hickness; the trend has been important enough, in the national imagination, to produce a string of ersatz hick presidents and an ongoing romance of backwardness, complete with a generic "country" accent that takes features of old Southern cracker speech and processes them through movies and TV series. The good-old-boy stance is not rural, but it is anti-urban, and anti-suburban, and evidently has a hold on our minds. Looking at Pete, you would never guess that he was born in Nairobi, Kenya, the son of missionaries, and grew up in Africa and California.

He asked, "How do you think the world's gonna end?"

"I don't know," I said. "I think it'll happen after I'm dead, anyway."

"No," he said, shaking his head, one cheek filled with tobacco. "It's gonna happen while I'm alive. There's gonna be a race war, against niggers, spics and the Jewish people. And I'm gonna be ready."

We went inside. Pete sat in a comfortable chair, chewing tobacco, his rifle close to hand. Ed and Mary Ruth were on the sofa. Mary Ruth had had a bad fall which led to partial paralysis, and, as part of her therapy, she was building a little ideal American town from bits of plastic and yarn that you buy through the mail. She had half a dozen buildings up already, on a shelf next to the TV. Now she was working on a flower shop. When she gets it finished, Ed said he wanted to mount the whole town on a board covered with Astro-Turf and contribute it to the church for display there.

Ed was in charge of channel-surfing. We were waiting for his favorite show, starring Chuck Norris as a Texas lawman. But first, a TV movie concerning a miracle and its misuse by an unscrupulous preacher. One of the main characters, a black woman (the organist), warned, "Anything that comes from God can be dangerous in the wrong hands." Next to my chair, on a table, was a slip of paper with a swastika. I watched it, out of the corner of my eye, for some time, then finally reached over, trembling slightly, and picked it up. "Fight Crime...," it read, "Deport Niggers." I've seen a thousand swastikas, but this one felt different. It meant what it said, on that very evening. Beneath it was a copy of *The Turner Diaries*, a best-selling novel about a militant cadre of white Americans who lynch Jews, kill blacks and blow up buildings. Sitting in my easy chair, I wondered if there weren't some way I could steal across the room, slip into the TV, take the organist by the hand and spirit her away.

Eventually Chuck Norris came on. The plot concerned a lunatic whom Chuck had put in prison — and who had escaped, determined to wreak terrible vengeance on everyone who had wronged him (a long list) and, in the end, on Chuck himself. A jowly, sweaty man, the killer was also an explosives expert. Over the course of the program he would incinerate a number of people; each time, as his eyes widened and his finger neared the fatal button, he quoted Scripture. His final act was to blow up the entire neighborhood where he had been a boy, a typical affluent suburban street with nice houses on quarter-acre lots. He blew the houses up one by one, an immense conflagration, and the whole neighborhood burned.

O N SUNDAY MORNING Ed, Mary Ruth and I put on our church clothes, crossed the muddy pathway and entered a strange building shaped like an igloo — the church. The service began with singing and dancing. Then each family took its turn standing before the congregation, singing a song, after which each member, beginning with the youngest and ending with the father, would step forward and give thanks to Yahweh. They would give thanks for the community, for the feeling of God's love, for a new dress. Often a speaker would weep, with embarrassment, pride and sometimes, it seemed to me, out of gratitude for being able to weep.

Many gave thanks that a young man who had been hit in the face by a swinging log had not been hurt more badly, for it was clear God had protected him. And when it came to be his own turn, this thin, laconic boy with the swollen face and the scabs could hardly express his thanks to everyone around him, many with tears in their eyes. His jaw still painful, he could hardly stammer out his thanks to God.

Many also gave thanks that another young man had decided

to marry and return to stay in Elohim City. The community's greatest fear is that the teenagers will move outside, where there are jobs and new faces — that they will choose to live in what is called here "the world" and so relinquish something of their share in the Covenant.

After the family testimonies, a young man posted himself by the main entrance with an assault rifle while someone from each family marched forward to receive the family's flag. These representatives joined in a rigid circle. Jim Ellison was there for the Family of Ellison, in his fatigues and blue scarf, wearing knives and, just for this ceremony, a straight flat sword in a red scabbard. The ceremony affirmed each tribe and recognized everyone's roots in the Torah and their special role in prophecy.

After more music, the children were gathered together on benches. People at Elohim City speak far more of family than of Yahweh. Every resource is directed at serving the children, who make up about half or more of the population and give their compound the air of a playground or summer camp. In practice, every adult is a parent to every child. The children always have someone older whom they can talk to about their problems, someone who will gladly listen. Mothers and fathers strain to be home for all three meals, to put the kids to bed and to get them up in the morning. Ed says the children understand the theology of the community even more rapidly than do the adults.

John Millar turned to the children, who by squeals and general acclamation brought burly James Ellison up from his chair. In folksy tones Ellison sidled into what I slowly realized was the Parable of the Loaves and the Fishes. He told it well. He emphasized that it had been a young boy who gave Jesus the loaves and fishes (John 6:8; in Matthew and Mark it was the disciples). Ellison concluded: "If you do whatever you do to help your mama and daddy or your brothers and sisters or your friends, all these might seem like little things but they're not. They're what it's all about. So remember that even if you're little, you can give a lot, and you can bless other people."

After their service the children left, and it was time for me to preach. The three teens made it through "Fighting the Beast," and I walked to a small lectern. I couldn't preach from Scripture. I don't know Scripture well enough. The only parable I can recall without effort is that of the prodigal son, my father's favorite. (He liked preaching from parables, in a mixed style all his own, one heavily influenced by black technique but usually directed at white Northerners.) I didn't want to preach on the Parable of the Prodigal Son in part because that story concerns God's forgiveness and I preferred not to preach, in this setting, about forgiveness.

I didn't want to preach at all, but I hate to be impolite, and I also felt a faint obligation not to remain silent.

I fashioned a sermon from real stories. I took them from my last book, and it surprised me how easily I could take years of work trying to find out true stories and just boil them down to parables. But the process occurred naturally and needed only a few minutes' thought. I told three parables about ethnic identity and nationalism — from Bulgaria, Turkey and Uzbekistan. Each case had its own set of variables. In each, distinct solutions were tried. When solutions didn't work, the result was terror, pain and bloodshed.

I ended with the Parable of the Uzbeks, in which an ethnic majority is ruled by an allegedly universalist ethnic minority (the Soviet Russians) for decades. The majority, that is, the Uzbeks, separates itself into truculent localisms to preserve autonomy, only to find, upon independence, that each locality distrusts the others and the nation refuses to build itself. According to the Uzbeks, I preached, "the problem is that, if anything bad happens, crime or whatever excuse people might want, then the neighborhoods are going to go against the neighborhoods, and there won't be any way to stop that. And that's the fear they live with now. And that's my third and last parable."

When I had finished my sermon the congregation at Elohim City stood and applauded. I begged them to sit down. I was out of breath and tried to hide next to Ed, who smiled in support. Reverend Millar nodded his head thoughtfully, then made some appreciative remarks, in his rich and grave voice, about the different histories of people and how fascinating these are, about "footprints in the sands of time," which led, willy-nilly, to his recalling (in German and English) something Adolf Hitler once said about "Blood and Land." My sermon had brought the phrase to mind. Perhaps I should have said, though I didn't, and it might not have made any difference: *No, these things truly happen. People's lives drain away in the mud and rubble. These are not stories; these are not parables.* But that would have been like saying, There are no angels, and you won't be saved.

in all directions and sh
ahhhhhhhhh.

so brief,

Loss of breath.

QUEENS ROAD CENTRAL, HONG KONG

Leo Ou-fan Lee

I FOUND MYSELF ON QUEENS ROAD CENTRAL the day before July 1, 1997, when Hong Kong was formally "returned" to China, or "handed over" as English newspapers described it, or, in American, when it "reverted." A pop song from a few years ago predicted this loss in a scene on the street where I stood:

QUEENS ROAD West and Queens Road East
They all merge into Queens Road Central
Why is there no palace on Queens Road East?
Only crowds of people on Queens Road Central.

A royal friend on the back of a coin
Forever young, her name is Queen
She follows me everywhere in my business run
Her face has no expression but earned reputation

Friends, saying bye-bye, going far away from this city
We will rely on a Great Comrade to provide us with a new vision

This judicious friend looks friendly
So he decrees that there'll be horse racing twice a week
And common folks must run fast to reach the end
You must have money to become the citizen of a big country

Emptiness is lust, and lust is empty

Friends, saying bye-bye, going far away from this city
We will rely on a Great Comrade to provide us with a new vision

There'll be railways and subways, public houses and taxis
And for directions it remains for the asking

Emptiness is lust, and lust is empty ...

Queens Road was the first street which the British colonists built after they set foot on the island as a result of the Opium War (1839–1840). Expectedly, it was named after Queen Victoria. This crowded thoroughfare was laid out along the Victoria harbor in a generally East-West direction, before the shoreline itself was pushed further down the sea by the massive landfill. Queens Road is now an "inland" street, rather narrow and extremely crowded at its Central section, and sheltered by the modern skyscrapers that form Hong Kong's breathtaking harbor skyline.

Queens Road Central conveys a different atmosphere than it used to: the street has lost much of its old glory, and its old buildings are so dwarfed by the nearby new high-rises that it now looks like a crowded back alley. The impression is reinforced by the many small sidestreets and narrow alleyways that link up to it, some serving as crowded bazaars for cheap merchandise. As one walks further east, Queens Road winds down, in fact, into a narrow alleyway itself, flanked on both sides by old curiosity shops that may, depending on one's mood and imagination, still conjure up Old Hong Kong.

I had walked all over the old harbor area along Queens Road East with a young woman friend from the United States. In addition to playing host, I was seeking "inspiration" for my first novel, a romantic story set in old Hong Kong and Shanghai. After a couple of hours of retracing old footsteps, I was utterly exhausted: in present-day Hong Kong, it takes both time and energy even to indulge in nostalgia. I was hot, thirsty and hopelessly depressed. The sentimental tour had somehow soured my mood, but I was unsure of the cause. Despite frequent trips to Hong Kong and a year of teaching there some twenty years ago, I cannot claim to be "local." My sudden urge to act as if I could undoubtedly stemmed from a faint desire to be close to the island's real residents, whose predetermined historical fate I have come to share.

It began to drizzle, and the uncooperative weather brought more rain showers later on. Desperately wanting to cheer myself up, I took my friend to visit Shanghai Tang, a fashionable boutique with a playful Orientalist decor in a sidestreet off Queens Road Central. We must not have looked touristy enough to attract the salesclerk's attention. I was sweating heavily, ill at ease though for no apparent reason. As we walked out, I was having difficulty making my way through the usual crowd of pedestrians, while my young friend was already darting forth excitedly like a true tourist. After a drink at a nearby waterhole, I said good-bye with some faint excuse and decided to wander alone.

As it began to rain I sought shelter in another plain-looking store nearby — only to realize after I walked in that it was Wing On, the legendary department store first established in the early 1920s. It now looked rather dilapidated. The shoppers were all local people, mostly men and women from the lower-middle class who tiredly gazed at the on-sale merchandise. In a matter-of-fact tone (speaking Cantonese to conceal my visitor's identity), I asked a plain-looking saleswoman to find any shirt that might fit my collar size: nothing fancy, I told her, just a plain blue shirt. Perhaps it was a delayed reaction to the treatment at Shanghai Tang, which presumably caters to both local customers and Western tourists who want to look purposefully "Oriental."

It was at that moment, as I left the store with my new shirt to face the crowd again on Queens Central, that the lyrics of this once popular song came to my mind. I took out the change the saleswoman had just given me and indeed found Her Majesty the Queen's face on the back of a coin: I saw a young visage (Queen Elizabeth, not the young Victoria of the Opium War years), tranquil-looking, blank. The face reminded me of the shoppers' faces, devoid of desire or excitement. Just a few days away from the Big Day, the local residents looked strangely unaffected, if not forlorn. Perhaps it is not so strange after all, because the "friends going far away" were already gone and those who remained were resigned to their fate.

One could still detect a festive atmosphere on Queens Road Central from the mushrooming banners that were displayed amid the omniscient shop signs — red banners displaying the Chinese phrase "Tomorrow can only be better," together with a toy-like white dolphin jumping (for joy?) through a rubber ring. I first thought that they were advertisements for a new aquarium, only to be told later that white dolphins are a precious species found only in the nearby oceans, hence a mascot for Hong Kong. (They are dying of water pollution caused by the construction of the new airport.)

NOSTALGIA MAY BE AN EMOTION reserved for old colonists. I come from a different background: when I first started teaching in Hong Kong in 1970 as a young instructor, I was a radical leader who spoke at student rallies and posted anti-colonial slogans outside my office door. I also looked "down" on Queens Road Central, where the fashionable bourgeoisie went shopping at swanky places like Wing On, Lane Crawford and Dragon Seed; there was, I recall, even a store called The Swank Shop. Thirty years later, the same old Queens Road looks rather cheap, like the Wing On department store, and even more congested with double-decker buses, taxis and, yes, "only crowds of people" and "no more palaces."

There has never been a Buckingham Palace in Hong Kong. A century ago British colonialism displayed all its architectural might in Shanghai, especially along the Bund, not in Hong Kong. The colonial buildings on the island — the Governor's Mansion, the Legislative Council Building, the Court Offices — are not striking. They are overshadowed by the commercial skyscrapers that have shot up in recent years near the Admiralty, west of Queens Road. Shielded behind Hong Kong's new skyline, Queens Road Central has become the quaint back-alley reminder of a colonial past long overtaken by rampant capitalism. To make the irony even more poignant, today's native Chinese capitalists are far ahead of British colonials in the race to become the new "patriotic" leaders, while fervently pledging allegiance to the socialist fatherland. It is this elite of native capitalists who have become Hong Kong's new overlords, leading the "silent majority" with confident patriarchal authority.

The lifestyle of my Chinese literary friends seems worlds apart from this financial elite. Avoiding expensive restaurants on top of world-class hotels, my friends would gather at local eateries for dim sum and "tea-drinking." One such place, Luk Yu, hidden on a nearby sidestreet, has become a local legend. Its regular customers, all locals, insisted that the interior be preserved as if it were from the 1930s — with ceiling fans, little lamps, wooden tables and chairs, spittoons for decoration and waiters who have worked there since its inception. In some ironic way, the waiters' rudeness to outsiders is taken to be a reinforcement of anti-colonial localism. However, in all the times I've been there, I've never been treated like a native; I am merely the guest of a native, my friend who is the editor of a famous outspoken journal. My most recent experience, after a few years' absence, was quite embarrassing. Walking up Queens Road Central, I missed the sidestreet and could not find the place, and once inside I was kept waiting by the door until my friend arrived, half an hour late. It suddenly occurred to me that perhaps the waiters, hearing me speaking Mandarin with another friend from the Mainland, mistook me for a "comrade" from China.

I WAS TOLD BY SOMEONE who worked for the Hong Kong government that all street names in Hong Kong, including Queens Road, will remain unchanged to avoid confusion. But won't anyone mind the constant colonial reminders? Wouldn't it be politically correct to change a few names too blatant for comfort, such as Prince Edward Road, Queen Victoria Street or even Queens Road? Wouldn't the Chinese government insist on the time-honored principle of *"zhengming"* — or "correcting names"? Indeed the new principle from Deng Xiaoping, the Great Comrade, seems to be working, at least on Hong Kong's streets. We now have "one country, two systems" — one with streets named after Chinese geography, the other after British royalty and colonial governors. It was a matter of practicality, explained my Hong Kong government informant, who happens to be British: "If you change street names, you may as well make all the Hong Kong vehicles drive on the right. Can you imagine the chaos? Or would you prefer that all the vehicles on the Mainland drive on the left?"

As I walked down Queens Road Central in the continuing drizzle, my depression was temporarily lifted when I saw hordes of young people crowded into a small square (called Queens Statue Square), their makeshift tents sheltering numerous stalls displaying an army of slogans and pamphlets in both Chinese and English. This political demonstration was billed as an "arts fair" — with the Cantonese word for "fair" serving as an international pun, signifying both "exhibition" and "ruins." I circled around the square a few times before plunging in and buying everything I could lay my hands on. In the course of this peculiar shopping spree, somebody at a small stand handed me a pen and asked me to write anything I could think of on a piece of hanging cloth. I thought of drawing a dying dolphin or putting down a funny phrase or a verbal pun, but eventually a literary muse came to my aid, and I wrote down a simple sentence in Chinese: "The spirit of Eileen Chang comes here for a visit." Eileen Chang was perhaps modern China's finest novelist, a Shanghai writer whose stories were often set in Hong Kong half a century ago and who achieved legendary status among Chinese readers every-where even before her death in Los Angeles. At that moment of epiphany, I knew that my own novel must be something of a sequel to one of her famous stories, "Love in the Fallen City."

Of all the world's cities with a sizable Chinese population, only in Hong Kong can you have a field day if you are a bilingual observer like me who makes a daily habit of negotiating between Chinese and English: the entire city is a semiotic spectacle of visual images and wordplays dis-played in an endless stream of shop signs, advertisements and even polit-ical slogans. In a sense, this "arts fair" on the eve of the takeover was but another dramatic extension of Hong Kong's semiotic energy, yet it also had, in the drizzle, the aura of shared historical awareness: this was the last time to enjoy such a gathering on the square, and friends who'd cho-sen to be there might as well make merry while it lasted, for tomorrow — for better or worse — would be another day.

Emptiness is lust, and lust is empty.

MATHILDE

John Brenkman

Fouqué succeeded in this mournful transaction. He was spending the night alone in his room with his friend's body when, to his great surprise, he saw Mathilde enter. A few hours earlier he had left her ten leagues out of Besançon. Her look and her eyes were wild.

"I want to see him," she said.

Fouqué hadn't the heart to speak or to rise. He pointed to a big blue cloak on the floor; what remained of Julien was wrapped up in it.

She dropped to her knees. The memory of Boniface de La Mole and Marguerite de Navarre gave her, no doubt, a superhuman courage. Her trembling hands undid the cloak. Fouqué turned his head.

He heard Mathilde walk hurriedly about the room. She lit several candles. By the time Fouqué had the strength to look at her, she had set Julien's head on a little marble table and was kissing it on the brow.

Mathilde followed her lover to the tomb he had chosen for himself. A great number of priests escorted the coffin, and unbeknownst to everyone, alone in her carriage draped with black, she bore on her lap the head of the man she had loved so dearly....

Having stayed behind with Fouqué, she insisted on burying her lover's head with her own hands. Fouqué nearly went mad with grief over this.

Through Mathilde's good offices, the rough cave was ornamented at great expense with marbles carved in Italy.

Mme de Rênal kept her promise. She made no attempt whatsoever on her life; but three days after Julien, she died while embracing her children.

— STENDHAL, *The Red and the Black*
trans. Lloyd C. Parks

So ENDS THE RED AND THE BLACK. Julien Sorel is executed for having tried to kill his former lover, Mme de Rênal, after she denounces him in a letter dictated by her priest to purify her adulterous soul. When the father of Mathilde de La Mole receives the letter, Julien's ambitions are shattered. Mathilde, who is pregnant, has only just persuaded her father to accept her marriage to his brilliant young secretary and launch him on a military and political career. Julien flees Paris to Verrières and enters the church where Mme de Rênal is praying. "He fired a shot and missed; he fired a second shot; she fell." Mme de Rênal recovers from her wounds and is filled with remorse for writing the letter; Julien seals his fate at the trial by confessing, "My crime is abominable, and it was *premeditated*."

I generally hate endings and easily forget them. My memory usually stays stuck on some twisted moment or dangling sequence out in the middle of the story somewhere, something the ending fails to answer to. I have to go back after even just a few months and reread a novel's last ten or twenty pages to recall how it all came out. Happy, neat, symbolic, perfectly ironic endings — there are so many ways to ruin a novel.

The spectacular endings of movies are worse yet. Even daring films have this problem. Godard's *Contempt* had a revival recently in a luscious color print that made its heart-stopping cruelties all the more unbearable. Fascinated with car crashes, which he elevated to a poetic indictment of contemporary life, Godard ends *Contempt* with one. But nothing "ends" the story more powerfully than the moment much earlier when the hero insists that his lover, Brigitte Bardot, ride alone in the car with a leering Jack Palance. His nonchalant and indifferent gesture means nothing less than rejection to her, and her love dies on the spot. Godard has made great films because he does not confuse the art of the cinema with that of the novel; he keeps the storyline thin and lets a gesture or look, an image or the exchange of a few words, do the work.

The Red and the Black is as intricate as a novel gets, and its ending pulls all the threads of its characters and settings, romance and social commentary, back together in a dense weave of aftermath. Stendhal's work has inspired far-reaching reflections by Lukács, Auerbach, Irving Howe, René Girard, Fredric Jameson and Franco Moretti. It is a linchpin of the 20th-century understanding of 19th-century European fiction. My earliest reading of the novel piqued my first interest in that critical tradition, and the novel and the criticism have nourished each other ever since. I've recently read it again, by chance around the time I saw *Contempt,* but the interpretive perspectives I've relied on before haven't quite worked. The obvious problems with the male-centered perspective of the *Bildungsroman* and with the established approaches to class and politics do not adequately explain why the novel seems to have changed. The problem lies elsewhere I've realized. I don't identify with Julien, I identify with Mathilde. But what can it mean to identify with a haughty, capricious, aristocratic heiress who loves her doting father and ends up carrying her lover's severed head cradled against her pregnant belly?

*I*DENTIFICATION IS THE WEAK LINK in modern criticism. Everyone knows that identifying with the hero or heroine is as basic to reading as fascination with plot or delight in language and ideas. Yet it remains relatively unexamined, relegated to a mix of personal associations and mechanical models that catalogue types of heroes. Personal associations stream off our responses to all manner of situations and characters, central or peripheral, but identification ultimately has to lock into the *form* of the novel as we read. Such identification is thus inevitably tied to the main character. The early Lukács, unfettered by the now fixed idea that the "narrator" "observes" the hero or heroine as a separate individual, saw novelistic writing itself as an act of identification: the author projects his or her own subjectivity into story and language in the creation of the hero, but something of that subjectivity splits off, through irony typically, into an estranged awareness of the hero's limits *and* of the powerlessness of this awareness to change the hero's horizon of decision and action.

Stendhal writes himself into Julien and beyond to achieve that disjointed unity of action and understanding, desire and reflection, as fully as any novelist of his time. *The Red and the Black* gives form to what Lukács thought of as the hero's effort to realize himself and enact whatever value he holds supreme in a world arranged against supreme values and the individuals who pursue them.

On the face of it this leaves no room for identifying with Mathilde in the strong sense of a form-disclosing identification. But here is where Stendhal's extraordinary ending comes into play. Julien's project is stopped in its tracks the moment he shoots Mme de Rênal, and Stendhal devotes the closing chapters of *The Red and the Black* to a different drama. As desire and action are lost to Julien, they are taken up by the three characters who attempt to save him, Mathilde, Mme de Rênal and his friend Fouqué. Julien himself is left to witness the sacrifices each of them is ready to make on his behalf. Fouqué, a woodcutter, proposes to spend all the money he has to arrange for Julien's escape. "'What a sublime gesture for a provincial landowner!' thought Julien. 'How much saving, the result of how much petty haggling, that used to make me blush when I watched him do it, he is willing to sacrifice for me. None of those handsome young men I saw at the Hôtel de La Mole who read *René* would ever do anything so ridiculous.'"

Mathilde leaves Paris and comes to Verrières disguised as a peasant. She throws herself into trying to sway and bribe jailers and the powerful Abbé de Frilair to gain Julien's freedom. On her arrival at the prison, Julien "abandoned himself joyously to his love for Mathilde. It was madness, greatness of soul, everything that is most uncommon."

Mme de Rênal, too, risks all. She writes to all thirty-six jurors pleading for an acquittal and then squanders her respectability altogether by defying her husband and going to see Julien after the verdict. When she enters his cell, thirty pages after his joyous reunion with Mathilde, Julien declares, "'You know that I have always loved you, that I have never loved anyone but you.'... Never had he been so madly in love." She wants to help him appeal his sentence and knows that her visits will turn her forever into "a heroine of anecdotes." What she could not do when she and Julien were lovers she has now done in the hopes of saving him:

> *"The limits of strict modesty have been crossed.... I am a woman without honor. True, it was for you...."*
>
> *Her voice was so sad that Julien embraced her, with a happiness entirely new to him. It was no longer the intoxication of love; it was utmost gratitude he felt. He had just become aware, for the first time, of the full extent of the sacrifice she had made for him.*

The trajectory that would make this Mme de Rênal's novel or Mathilde's is there in outline throughout, invisible until you look back across the story from these final chapters in which *their* desires and efforts become manifest. The conflicting lines of identification — with Julien, Mme de Rênal, Mathilde — give the novel a complexity that is not easily rounded off.

THE DRAMA OF SACRIFICES, it seems to me, shows the fault-lines. Certainly, as Stendhal signals more than once, Julien grows during his last months in prison. In recognizing Fouqué's nobility, Mathilde's heroism and Mme de Rênal's self-sacrifice, he discovers the capacity for gratitude missing from the ambition, "softheartedness" and "wiliness" that have always guided him. But something is awry when he lets go of Mathilde and reaffirms his lost love for Mme de Rênal. This true love is suspect, for Julien finds himself and his desire only in the other's willingness to sacrifice herself for him.

The death-tinged reconciliation of Julien and Mme de Rênal dominates the last pages of the novel. Julien loses his feeling for Mathilde, except in the *malaise moral* which nags him for being bored by her even as she is ruining herself to save him. Because his own heroic striving has been annihilated, he is indifferent to hers. "In his heart ambition was dead; another passion had risen from its ashes. He called it remorse for having attacked Mme de Rênal. He was, in fact, head over heals in love with her (*Il en était éperdument amoureux*)." Julien and Mme de Rênal indeed complete each other: they have inflicted symmetrical wounds on one another and felt identical remorse and now exchange mutual pardons and forgiveness. They reunite seeking harmony out of their recognition that they have each irreversibly missed the moment to give their love to the other.

The ending offers completion for readers starved for meanings — as well as for those in the habit of killing their appetite with irony. Julien is ready for the guillotine because he believes he deserves death for shooting Mme de Rênal, declaring before the court that "she had been like a mother to me." Meanwhile, she finds in his love for her the forgiveness she seeks: "Julien's raptures and his happiness proved to her how fully he pardoned her." What looks like a love which transcends guilt in forgiveness is actually fed by permanent guilt. Neither Mme de Rênal's remorse for writing the letter that prompted Julien's irreparable act nor Julien's remorse for the act he committed — "whether out of ambition or out of love for Mathilde" he is not sure — is truly overcome.

Mme de Rênal's declaration of love is in the language of piety: "I am nothing but love for you; or rather — the word 'love' is too feeble — I feel for you what I ought to feel for God alone: a mixture of respect, love, obedience." The happy couple is spared having to figure out what it would be like to live with *that*. What's awry in the novel's ending is this perfection itself. Julien and Mme de Rênal discover the courage to love one another only in the unreal space where it cannot be lived, the other-worldly imaginary created by the grim reality of Julien's impending execution. They inhabit a tableau full of symbols, Oedipus plus Christ: Julien walks to the scaffold filled with love for Mme de Rênal, and she dies spontaneously three days after the carpenter's son is buried in a cave.

M ME DE RÊNAL AND MATHILDE knew their own desire. Julien didn't know his until it was too late, and Mme de Rênal didn't act on hers until it was too late. Only Mathilde acts on what she knows and desires. That's why identification with her, playing against the identifications with Julien and Mme de Rênal, alters the perspective on the novel's tragedy, for Mathilde's love, laden though it is with aristocratic legends and mythologies, does not attain any symbolic fullness.

Even as she knows and enacts her love, it needs the reciprocal love and recognition Julien does not give. She is therefore bereft at the end. She does not look away from grief, even in the knowledge that Julien turned to Mme de Rênal, but returns to Fouqué's to see Julien's body and hold his head. When she puts his head on the marble stand and kisses his brow, the novel stirs up the grotesque. But in fact kissing a dead person you love is not grotesque, it's a simple act of love and remembrance. Even Stendhal perhaps cannot overcome the voyeurism or the disgust that accompanies the separation of touch and sight. Yet Mathilde's reality is decidedly not a tableau, symbolic or sensational; it is the reality of touch, which is why Stendhal makes her final act in the story burying "her lover's head *with her own hands*." She does not die into transcendence but lives on in mourning.

Before Julien died, he attempted to arrange Mathilde's future for her in an act that had more to do with his guilt than her well-being. She, after all, was willing to flee with him to an unknown future, had he chosen life and uncertainty over death and harmony. He insisted she have the baby in secret in Verrières, leave it behind in the care of Mme de Rênal, return to Paris the revered widow of a madman and marry some ambitious young man whose career she could foster. Stendhal, however, gives no hint of Mathilde's future in the closing pages or paragraphs. In declining to symbolize or even imagine her destiny — does she keep the baby or abandon it? does she return to Parisian society or flee it? does she pursue her happiness or withdraw from the world? — Stendhal gives his clearest affirmation to an identification with Mathilde. Unlike Julien and Mme de Rênal, she keeps making her life her own.

CIRCE'S PALACE

Anne McClintock

*I*T IS EVENING AND IT IS HOT. It is New York hot, ozone laced and electric. Here on the edge of the river, between the meatpacking district and the sprawl of the Department of Sanitation, two homeless figures bend over a brazier, casting shadows towards the line of men waiting patiently at a door. Above the crowd, a giant, orange V has been painted on the building, lurid and somehow obscene, like a crotch. Below the V, a white limo idles, its windows blank as a coffin.

I am writing a book on the sex trade and I've been told to check out the Vault, New York's premier S/M club. I've never been to the Vault, but I have a pretty vivid image of it anyway. A number of images, actually. In one, a woman hangs like a chrysalis from a hook, ringed by men in black leather. The men have corrugated stomachs and bullwhips. The woman is gagged, turning slowly on her hook. You know the picture. You know it already. Circe's palace, I think, where men have tusks and blood-rimmed eyes, where men are turned into swine.

I join the line of men descending the black stairway that leads down into the Vault. At the bottom of the stairs, I am stopped by a man checking bags. A dangling lightbulb floods my eyes so I can see nothing beyond his white face.

"Any weapons?" he asks.

"Weapons?" I ask.

He waves at a sign above the window:

LEAVE ALL WEAPONS OUTSIDE EXCEPT THE ONE GOD GAVE YOU

He gives me an affable wink, takes my fifteen dollars and I go into the Vault. The woman at the coat check is a sturdy blonde with stiff-looking hair the color of wheat. She's wearing a well-tailored cream suit, a cream satin blouse and a string of soft pearls round her neck. Not what I had been expecting. She smiles a large, lipsticky smile as she takes my bag.

"Will that be all?" she says in a friendly baritone and I look down and see hairy legs in stockings and big feet squeezed into a Cinderella pair of oyster, satin pumps.

"Have a good evening, dear," she says kindly, taking my dollar.

The Vault is a sepulchral cave with a bar in the middle lit by a single light. A catacomb of blackened alcoves leads off to the sides. Smoke hovers in the dim light above the bar, where a waitress is wiping glasses. The place has a fungoid smell like a cave or an old church. The air doesn't move and everything is black. The ceiling is black, like a midnight sky. The floors are black and even the couches and benches along the walls are black. It occurs to me that if I go to the ladies' room, the toilet paper will be black. As I cross the room to the bar, the floor has a stickiness that I prefer not to think about.

The joint's not jumping. At first glance, the place has a kind of somnolent squalor, a charged desolation. Groups of shadowy men hover in the corners, but it's hard to see anything at first. Near me, a few men hug the bar, their eyes sliding slowly round the room as if they are waiting for someone important to make an appearance. The middle floor is empty except for a roped off section like a boxing ring.

I make my way to the bar and ask for a glass of red wine, but the waitress shakes her head and smiles, wiping her cloth across the bartop. She looks perfectly ordinary.

"No alcohol," she says. "Soda, ginger ale, coke. What'll you have?"

"Why no alcohol?"

"So we can have full frontal," she says. "Full frontal means no alcohol. Department of Alcohol law. Also we don't allow no anal and no penetration. But we do allow masturbation," she hastens to add. "So you can release yourself. And fisting is, of course, allowed. With condoms. We have condoms and lube and an upstairs floor for transvestites," and she waves her dishcloth invitingly at a box of condoms sitting under the counter next to the vat of ice and the Vault T-shirts.

I perch on the edge of my stool, sipping my watery soda like a cabaret singer between sets, pretending to a nonchalance I don't remotely feel. I gaze sidelong about me and the room comes slowly into focus. There are video monitors in the corners playing the sort of things one sees on the Discovery Channel, close-ups of anteater's tongues cleaning out termite nests, bulbous sea-slugs swelling to fill the screen, crimson anenomes opening their frilled hearts, except that these are human organs pulsating slow-motion in a wet, pink light.

In the dimness I can't see much, but there's a slow, penumbral movement of men around the room. Every now and again a man detaches himself from the shadows and makes his way somewhere else. People seem to be moving about the room as if they've lost something, as if they can't remember what they've lost, but are looking for it anyway. The atmosphere is entranced, pacific, like a secret island marooned in an unmapped sea. And if I have nerved myself for the raw voltage of male power, I don't yet see it.

Then a man appears in a soft, red silk dress. He has a distracted air, as if he is looking for someone, as if, through some unfortunate error, his regrettably stolid body was originally destined for some other, more convincingly masculine man, and that this man is now also walking about the planet, also astonished, in a woman's form not intended originally for him; and if he could simply find this person, strolling about in his own lovely, lost and perfumed body, then the proper exchange might be made and everything righted.

From somewhere in the shadowy alcoves, a young man with a sleepy face passes in front of me. He's half-naked, wearing only a white T-shirt. He has a strangely meek and childish aspect, as if he's a small boy in pajamas off to bed. He looks befuddled and dreamy, as if he'd fallen asleep amongst the cushions watching TV; the flickering, blue images are still playing loosely over his face. He's sleepwalking; his childish penis has a limp innocence. I can almost see the grubby teddy bear under his arm as he disappears into one of the alcoves.

THERE'S A MOVEMENT AND SOMEONE IS CROUCHING near me, about a pace away. He has limp, brown hair parted neatly down one side and a vaguely hunched look as if he is trying to make himself smaller. He has a furtive, marsupial face, but he doesn't look at me. Instead, he dips his head towards one of my boots, keeping his eyes averted.

"Foot worship, Mistress?" he mumbles.

I'm stricken with nerves. What's the protocol? What are the rules? I don't know the game, haven't a clue, so I opt for inaction and look with interest past the man, as if I've just spotted someone really worth knowing across the room.

"Mistress?" he mumbles.

I ignore him, stiff with embarrassment.

He falls to his knees at a respectful distance and he remains there, hunched, as if praying. I pretend not to see him, not knowing what else to do. He scrambles to his feet, head bowed, gaze averted and backs slowly away, the way servants were obliged to leave a room in late Victorian England.

Welcome to the Vault. Welcome to Circe's palace, where men wear skirts and women are tops. This is not what I had been expecting.

It's very quiet here in this antechamber, subdued and almost churchy. Emboldened, I slip off my stool to do the rounds of the place and a man brushes slightly against me as I pass.

"Oh, excuse me, Madam," he mumbles, abject with apology, but he looks at me half-hopefully out the corner of his eyes.

"That's okay," I say, as if perfectly at ease, gazing into the middle distance again, but pleasant, careful not to catch his eye. The man moves off, his shoulders repentant, but five minutes later he's back and as he passes, he bumps ostentatiously into me.

"Oh, excuse *me*, Madam," he says, as if mortified by his body's effrontery.

"That's okay," I say again and as I move off, a woman nearby leans towards me.

"He wants you to cuss him out," she confides. "Don't apologize. Here women don't apologize."

So when he brushes past me again, I know what to do.

"Listen," I say, "If you touch me again without permission." I pause for effect. "If you *ever* touch me again."

"Sorry, Mistress. Sorry," he mumbles, a look of quiet elation on his face.

"Won't happen again," he says happily.

He moves off and three minutes later he's back, standing a few feet away. He waves a fumbling, apologetic hand towards his crotch, with a kind of helpless distaste as if he has just messed in his pants and I catch in his eyes a look of such beseeching, humiliated, hopeless yearning that I know again what he wants. He wants to be seen; he wants a witness. I turn away without looking.

And the women? There are a couple of dominatrixes chatting on a bench. One has long, black hair sweeping over her shoulders and a skin pale as an Irish fog. Her lips are purple and goth and her friend has crimson hair extensions. A few other women, coy and embarrassed, look like voyeurs from the bridge-and-tunnel crowd.

Then another man appears, giving me a caged-animal look as he passes. He is dressed, but his soft mouth has a vaguely indecent look, pink and mucous, as if it really belongs in a more secret part of his body. I notice his fly is undone: his penis is jutting out. It is furiously erect and red with a swollen head like a little fire hydrant. He drifts into one of the alcoves and I follow him in.

The boy with the sleepy face is naked on his back on the bare floor, his pants curled round his feet like a fallen diaper. His legs are crooked out to the sides and his T-shirt is scrunched up under his arms. An old man is watching him from a corner. The old man's penis is tiny, but the glans is fat and round like a constable's helmet. Sitting on a bench before the boy on the floor, thick thighs splayed, is a ponderous dominatrix in a black skirt and leather bra. She has a warm skin the color of coffee beans and huge, oily breasts and she seems sedate and motherly, with that vaguely absented expression on her face that women wear in supermarket lines or doctors' offices. As she leans towards the boy, breasts lolling and placid, her flesh creases over and over like a squeezed-out concertina. He gazes up at her, his eyes milky, his mouth slack with longing.

She might have been about to pat his bottom with talcum powder, except that he has a tense erection and she has taken off one of her shoes and is rubbing her stockinged foot up and down on his penis, up and down, rhythmic and perfunctory, rub-a-dub-dub, like a mother rocking a child to sleep. Except that he is about to come and his body shudders on the cold, bare floor and he arcs his head back and jerks once, and then twice, and then he comes on his stomach and lies there for a while as if he were dead.

Then he sits up dazedly and wipes a hand slowly down his face as if he is wiping away water or tears. He leans forward unsteadily and with the fastidious attention of a child learning to clean himself, he tears off a piece of kitchen napkin from the roll nearby and mops meticulously at his stomach. He pauses for a second, then clambers to his feet and hikes up his trousers. The old man watches him sadly from the corner. The boy stands unsteadily for a second, lost, then lifts his cheek to the woman, the way a sleepy child might lift his face to be kissed. But she has already turned away. The session is over.

*S*O, ULYSSES, WHAT DID YOU THINK, stung with salt and skin hunger, peeping through the scratchy bushes on the beach, gripping your flower, your magic moly? What did you think, when you saw your hairy men, mariners all, in their dainty frocks, in their flounced skirts, their mother's lipstick smeared on their faces, mincing down the green lawns of Circe's palace? Did you, too, long for a pretty, yellow bodice and soft stockings, the shimmer of blue silk against your penis? Was it your idea to change the story?

This is an extract from a forthcoming book, Skin Hunger: A Chronicle of the Sex Trade *(Jonathan Cape, 1998).*

Masochism, A Masque

Wayne Koestenbaum

T O RAIL against Disney is to say the obvious.

First I will rant about computers. Later I will discuss Times Square and masochism.

I hate computers, even though I am using one. Computers make people stupid.

I advocate the agrarian.

I telephone a chain bookstore. "What books by Harold Robbins do you have in stock?" I ask the salesclerk.

"Let me check the computer," he says, and puts me on hold.

Why not check the shelves?

The clerk comes back on the line to say that the computer only lists initials of first names. H. Robbins. There are hundreds of H. Robbins titles.

He says, "*Descent from Xanadu.* Is that by Harold Robbins?"

"I don't know," I say. "It doesn't sound like Harold Robbins."

"What about *Spellbinder. The Lonely Lady. Goodbye, Janette.*"

Things are looking up.

The clerk puts me on hold.

The clerk comes back to say "*Where Love Has Gone. Never Love a Stranger.*"

Happiness.

I'd like to register a complaint, however.

I expect quick service and I expect clerks to know their stock.

I want to defame chains.

"You sound like a Marxist," a writer said to me at a cocktail party. I was complaining about chains. I said, "I'm not a Marxist. I'm too ignorant of Marx to be a Marxist." She said, "You sound like a Marxist. That's refreshing."

Moments earlier in the conversation I'd offended her by complaining about elites. Turned out she belonged to the very elite I was criticizing.

Accidentally I'd spit a bit of smoked salmon onto my palm, and when I shook her hand, I think she could feel the fish fleck.

Yesterday I met a rich man. He moved slowly, though he is only forty. He moves slowly not because he is arthritic or tired, but because he is rich. He didn't wiggle his head nervously in every direction while he spoke. When I talk, I wiggle my head. This is because I am not rich. I am upper-middle class, the lower end.

Do you understand?

Times Square.

The men who walk into the few remaining porn shops are sometimes handsome. I want to engage them in conversation.

I am depressed to see the sexual history of Times Square erased.

I won't claim that Times Square was a utopia, but it was certainly important. See George Chauncy's *Gay New York*. See Sal Mineo's *Who Killed Teddy Bear?* See Joseph Cornell's diaries.

Alas, the Eros has closed, and the Adonis.

The Gap takes up some of the slack, but not enough.

The Disney Store takes up none of the slack, unless you bring your direst sexual fantasies into the store, or unless you adopt the following style: he or she who verbalizes the sexualized advances that commodities make on our imaginations and actions.

Dumbo is a sexualized commodity.

Other commodities that haunt me are books and countries: I have been alphabetizing my books and I have been planning trips to Florida and Sicily. In Miami I want to become more of a guy by getting a tan and relaxing. In Taormina I will seek echoes of the boys that Baron Wilhelm von Gloeden photographed. See Emmanuel Cooper's *Fully Exposed: The Male Nude in Photography*. See the turn of the century.

I have been thinking seriously about prostitutes. My favorite porn star is Max Grand. In a free gay mag he advertised: "Pornstar. Max Grand. In NYC 11/6 – 11/18. Nationwide Pager 310–298–3951." I may avail myself of his services and write at great length about the experience.

Max Grand is not a commodity. He is a male escort from El Salvador. His films include *Latin Tongues, Hot Springs Orgy, Leather Confessions, Chicago Meat Packers* and *Cut vs. Uncut*. He is a superstar.

In *Wet Warehouse #2* he has a lovely speaking voice and a desk job.

Last night I dreamed my students complained about my pedagogy. I was trying, in a huge lecture course, to discuss the difference between cleanliness and filth. I was faultily explaining the co-existence of dirty and clean in the work of Marianne Moore and Elizabeth Bishop. I said incoherently, "Moore's forms look clean but her metaphors are filthy." I was projecting slides of Renaissance paintings — closeups of fabric.

So what if I made my students cry?

Everything quickly devolved into a textbook case of sexual harassment, and the dream ended.

I have been thinking about sadomasochism. I have not been practicing it.

The difference between praxis and mimesis, my old favorite, is not a crux I shall belabor today.

A few leatherfolk I've recently met are among the nicest people in my circle. I feel at home with them. They wear interesting clothes. They talk casually about gear: "I'm wearing a cock ring today."

They don't talk about identity: "I am a sadist." They talk about scenes: "I did an interesting scene."

I did an interesting scene today. I stood in the vicinity of a commodity and ignored it.

I pretended a person was a commodity. I stared at the person, once my friend, and ignored his soul.

I imagined him dead.

I smiled at him while picturing him evacuated.

It is difficult to think outside the lure of commodities.

I mean clothes and books and prostitutes and photographs and neighborhoods and corporations.

This is not a lecture about commodities. I am hardly qualified.

See Guy Hocquenghem's *Homosexual Desire*, especially the chapter on the anus, capitalism and the family.

See the Guess ad campaign.

See Celine Dion.

See me. After class. For tips. On how to ignore commodities.

It is beginning to snow. I am beginning to remember the first short story I wrote, in 1976. I am beginning to forget my body.

My father saw Disney's *Fantasia* in Caracas, 1940. Or was it 1941? I romanticize the moment of him watching it. He saw it several times. It inspired him to want to become a musician. He took piano lessons. He conducted an orchestra, at least once, in college. He conducted the overture to *Don Giovanni*. Or so I remember him telling me. The memory is crucial yet vague.

In Caracas my father wanted to play Monopoly. He couldn't find it in the stores, or his father wouldn't buy it for him. I can't remember. So my father fabricated his own Monopoly board game. This proves his ingenuity. He was a self-starter.

I played Monopoly obsessively in fourth and fifth grade. My favorite color group contained Marvin Gardens. I loved owning cheap, easily conquered territories: Baltic Avenue.

For every lost tooth I received a silver dollar under my pillow.

I wanted to be rich and French. I called myself "Pierre."

I've nearly given up telling stories about myself.

I don't advocate the self. I advocate the body, an envelope for practices and impulses: a switchboard.

The switchboard contains soul.

Sometimes I man my switchboard. Sometimes my various replacements man it. Sometimes no one mans it.

Sometimes New York City mans it.

Those are exciting moments, though they also resemble drowning.

A person is a style.

I'm waging war against the homogenization of styles.

Get your hands off my switchboard.

I shall now talk about my brother.

I have many brothers.

Five of them visited this morning. I took them shopping. We bought veal stew meat and eggs and Windex.

Keep your heart clean.

That is what I tell my five.

It is Xmas and time to buy gifts for my five.

This is a year for bookbuying. I want to support the independents.

For Brother #1, I will buy *Valley of the Dolls*.

For Brother #2, Jamaica Kincaid's *My Brother*.

For Brother #3, a wine encyclopedia.

For Brother #4, *Discipline and Punish*.

For Brother #5, *The Elements of Style*.

Where shall we dine for Xmas supper?

Downtown.

On the river.

Porridge for the first course, the second and the third.

I want to starve the brothers.

Let them read but do not let them eat.

When we were young we had a tinsel Xmas tree. It came folded in a box. We unfolded it and surrounded it with gifts. Red balls hung from the fake silvery branches. I am certain that it was a fire hazard. It glittered in the room, beside the Heidegger.

We almost ate the Heidegger.

The wind whips through my room. The wind has a mission. It wants to cleanse my thought.

The wind is rattling through my brain. Do you hear? It whistles in the rafters, near the murder mysteries. I bought them at a chain.

Give fifty dollars to Children's Aid.

Don't mention it.

This Xmas, figure out why I'm in love with the aesthetic of autism, the aesthetic of incommunicado.

I admire writing that doesn't communicate, or that communicates blockage.

At the kosher deli the sight of a fat man eating a triple-decker sandwich dissuaded me from ordering a side dish of chopped liver.

Today I have listed the impediments to embodiment.

I do not want to stop.

I enjoy suspense. Harmonic suspension in Wagner, Strauss and Chopin is a history of masochism.

Wagner keeps your body distant from completion, so you may have the pleasure of interminable waiting.

The divergence between the left and the right hands, in a Chopin *morceau*, is an agent of masochism. The right hand's melodic figuration moving separately from the pulsations of the left is a catalyst of masochistic experience in the listener.

The right hand lags behind.

You want it to speed up, but it can't.

The first time I experienced the masochistic oscillation, I was listening to "Siegfried's Idyll."

Wrong. The first time I experienced a pulsation I'd call masochistic, I was observing a cut on a local thumb. The thumb was mine, but also not mine. The wound was the most beautiful object in the kitchen. The wound came from a juice glass, near the medicine bottle. Either the glass had a rough, broken edge, or another, veiled object, in the vicinity, ripped my skin.

The room around the cut on the thumb was dulcet and nonverbal.

The kitchen of the cut was off the dark dining room.

The cut was a sign of greatness.

If I could only live up to the cut — if I could only equal it!

See Gaston Bachelard's *The Poetics of Space*.

My hands are cold from trills.

When I trill, my fingers grow numb.

This is a trill, from C to C-sharp.

It sounds like a razor. It sounds like Emily Dickinson's "firmament."

To warm my fingers, I will stop writing.

My neurosystems' disturbed minutiae are the logical consequence of a shattered worldview.

If I could name the worldview and the cause of its shattering, I would be the master of my style.

As matters stand, I am merely its personal shopper. V̇

TESTIMONIO: ECHO OR NARCISSUS?

Hugo Achugar

*S*IC AMET IPSE LICET, SIC POTIATUR AMATO. I translate: "May he love as I do; may he, also in the same way, not be loved." The fulfillment of Echo's wish implicitly requires Narcissus' death. When Narcissus rejects the nymph Echo, she runs off and wastes away, until all that remains is the repetitive quality of her voice. He also rejects a young man, Aminias, whose plea for revenge is heard by Nemesis, and Narcissus is doomed. The rest of the story is well known: Narcissus falls in love with his own reflection in a pool, languishes as he contemplates himself and ends up metamorphosed into a flower. I find this story, with its many variations and interpretations, a suggestive backdrop for thinking about autobiography and Latin American *testimonio*.

Critics generally do not much distinguish autobiography, memoir and *testimonio*. Some, however, have emphasized that the *I* in *testimonio* is a collective subject, unlike the individual and personal *I* of autobiography. Though the *I* in *Rigoberto Menchu* or *A Runaway Slave* is of course an

individual (Rigoberta Menchu, Esteban Montejo), it is in effect present-
ed as the expression of a social subject. The *I* becomes representative. In
autobiography, by contrast, the individual *I* does not aspire to represent
some social or collective entity; indeed, the norms of autobiographical
writing make this nonrepresentative individual uniquely the source of the
story and the origin of the narration itself.

Behind the autobiographical norms is a Romantic notion of subjectivity, which acquires a kind of role-modeling function in the sense that
the autobiographically narrated life is typically valued not only because
it is individual but also because it is unique, exceptional, extraordinary.
Testimonio draws *its* norms from another Romantic notion, namely, that
the "people" are the true source of the narration. The romantic collectivity is variously associated with a group, class, community or nation.

The idea of representing the voice of the Other long enjoyed unques-
tioned legitimacy, but more recently has come to be seen as something
dangerously close to illegitimate appropriation. Suspicion of notions of
authenticity, veracity and legitimacy affects not only testimonial discourse, with its aspirations to representativeness and agency, but also
contemporary ethnography and journalism. Autobiography still enjoys
an unexamined tolerance towards its fictional tendencies, its shadowy
overlap of truth and invention, fact and embellishment. The autobiographical *I* is constructed in the writing process much like a fictional
character, yet is inevitably accepted as a real person. *Testimonio*, by contrast, immediately loses its validity if suspected of being untrue or apoc-
ryphal, falling into the genre of romance or fiction and losing its most
essential claim to being a document, evidence and witness, a counterhegemonic narration of history.

I AND THOU, I AND THE OTHER, US AND THEM — these categories have been a powerful force in Western thought for centuries. The Greeks' preoccupation with barbarians (remember Xenophon's
Anabasis); the European response to the fact that the New World had

inhabitants (remember Montaigne, et al.); and the current habit of representing the Third World as the contemporary Other — these are just highlights in an old and still meaningful story of hate and racism. The discursive construction of the *I* and the *We* keeps trying to ground itself, dialogically, through its image of an Other, those who are different, Them.

Testimonio invariably sees itself as counterhegemonic because it is giving written form to the testimony of an Other, a person and collectivity that have suffered the role of barbarian: outside our language, our laws, our values, our culture. Traditionally biography and autobiography in Latin America — and elsewhere I assume — have ignored the Other and dealt exclusively with the hegemonic role model. A third trend has begun to appear in autobiographies that privilege ordinary experience and "partial histories." It's possible that these new autobiographies are evidence that new social groups are gaining access to writing and print, *or* that neoliberal cynicism has simply found its latest tactic in search of new publishing markets.

To pose the questions in this way assumes there is a neat distinction between hegemony and counterhegemony, and that these categories will sort out the political and cultural significance of the various forms of life-writing. I am not so sure, because of two problems. First, the Other has not always been the same. The Other at the time of the Conquest was the "savage," whether noble or cannibalistic. That older Other certainly remains present in the new Other insofar as Otherness involves being silenced, censored or repressed. The Other is historical, and whoever holds the power to command the political and social discourse determines and designates who the Other is: immigrants, political dissidents, gays as well as CIA agents, sandinistas and/or contras. The problem in Latin America is that power is always in the same hands!

The second problem is one that haunts our current fascination with *testimonio* and our faith in its political meaning. For doesn't the narcissistic impulse so obvious in autobiography also reveal itself in *testimonio*? The counterhegemonic defense of the Other — socially or politically oppressed groups, women, gays, indigenous peoples and so on — manifests the desire to confirm what the committed writer and the avid reader already know and believe, and so reaffirms what they already believe *themselves* to be. How different is this from the self-love of autobiography?

D O I DARE SUGGEST THAT DEFENDERS of the Other might be motivated by, or desire, the self, the sameness of identity? Worse yet, is it possible to imagine that Rigoberta Menchu, Esteban Montejo and Jesusa Palanares — icons of social solidarity — have individualistic desires, not just the desire to give the silent and oppressed a voice?

Ovid's story offers parallels to clarify the questions I am raising. The relevance of Narcissus to *testimonio* does not lie in his relation to his own image, as in autobiography, so much as in the relation between Echo and Narcissus. Narcissus looking fondly at his image is writing the watery page of his autobiography, but his voice, too, is doubled, and that's another story. Juno jealously punished the nymph Echo by depriving her of the ability to initiate speech, leaving her able only to repeat, incompletely, what others say. Yet, in echoing Narcissus, Echo declares her love for him. In *testimonio* the writer (Miguel Barnet, Elena Poniatowska, Elizabeth Burgos-Debray) sets up a dialogue like the one between Echo and Narcissus. The sympathetic writer, the friendly literate, repeats — in love — what the Other says. The repetition is supposedly the mirroring of an alien discourse, the doubling of a repressed oral testimony. But the repetition is not exact. The *testimonio* writer is again like Echo who, in repeating only what she can, changes the meaning of Narcissus' words, turning them into her own discourse of love. The person who gives the testimony is like Narcissus: without his presence no *image* (of the oppressed collectivity) could be crafted, and at the same time without Echo's voice Narcissus' would not become dialogue; without the voice of the friendly writer, Rigoberta Menchu or Esteban Montejo wouldn't exist for the learned or literate world. It is the writer in love who makes the informant's discourse possible and gives it the form and significance we instantly recognize as *testimonio*.

ered by la
d po
veek after his mother
of mine dreamed
snow-white wolf. He

ESSAY

THE GOOD PERSONS OF GERMANY

Bodo Morshäuser

1.

Why is it that conversations with skinheads and right-wing extremists aren't tiresome while those with their opponents are? I talked with skinheads without any problem. The only problems were in my mind, until I took a step toward them and said what I wanted to.

The tiresome conversations were with other people. There was hardly a discussion about right-wing extremism without the tacit or explicit agreement among those who were talking that they were more politically educated than those who were being talked about and not participating in such discussions. When I talked about my research to discussion groups, people readily said that what I was doing was important. I felt like running away from that automatic knee-jerk reaction. Those declaring that my research was some special achievement had themselves made no effort to understand people who tend to extreme right-wing opinions; they'd much rather condemn them wholesale. I told them they were wrong. *Those* conversations were grueling. The ones with skinheads were often funny, because no one verbalized cleverly around an issue but talked straight.

While I was doing my research, the so-called educated people seemed stupid to me. I've hardly ever heard more stupid talk on the topic than from people who could brag about their education and special expertise in this and that field. An introverted, half-educated babbling can wrap around days that begin with café au lait and end with Chianti. And I felt that such endless talk without any real grasp of the subject simply kept the know-it-alls from having to look at the reality they were judging. They related to that reality only by putting forth their cultivated prejudices at the opportune moment.

The question always implicit in the discussions is how to proceed against people who think differently. The enmity is considered self-evident, and the only question is *how*. The idea of listening to strangers before proceeding against them is foreign to these intellectual warriors. Consequently, the praise I got for having talked with skinheads clashed with the fact that those enthusiasts could not bear it when I told them what the world looks like in the eyes of others. These intellectuals were usually ten years older than me, children of the war generation. They felt they bore responsibility and stressed their aversion to the oppositional young people. Not a trace of insight into the fact that young right-wing extremists too are our children.

The best-known slogan of the young people — the children of the postwar children — is *We are proud to be Germans*. They know this declaration will provoke antagonism, which is quite possibly their reason for making it. They know they're saying something forbidden.

And how are they answered? *For the sake of the Germans'*

victims, no one should be proud to be a German. The "proud one," noticing that the others are ashamed, then backs them into a corner which they can't get out of except by offending him with an exaggeration: "Nazi!" — in response to which he too exaggerates, and so begins the dunce-dialogue of automatic reflex reactions.

Such conversations almost never end by getting the other to reflect. On the contrary, the positions harden and become entrenched. If in the beginning there were two people talking with one another, by the end there are two people insulting each other, if not beating each other up. The one has informed the other he is the enemy, and both sides are convinced they're right.

In an often repeated, nearly absurd scenario, some teenager proclaims his pride and highly educated, grown-up people respond by going through all the motions, from good advice to a verbal smack. What a success for the teenager!

Why does this keep happening? It's no coincidence, but a precondition, that the topic neither side can negotiate is connected with their Germanness and Germany. Why do so many find it impossible to allow others to be proud of their origin? And why do these others need to claim they are proud? Those words have their effect because there are so many who are ashamed of being German. Why are they ashamed? Why do some of us deny belonging to this land?

2.

Finally the war was over. The German youth who'd set off to expand the Reich came back defeated men and women. There were no heroic deeds to chronicle. They cried over the ruins in their own country, cleared them away and had children. They forgot what they lost in their youth and started over "from scratch." Later their children asked about the time that was never talked about, and usually received evasive answers. They noticed that they had to drag every word out of their parents by force, and that their questions touched a sore spot in their survivor-parents. The questions increasingly became assertions and felt unjust to many of the older people. A million times the relation between the war generation and their children cracked. *Ihre Kinder*, Your Children, as one of the first German bands called itself, then lived out their parents' unacknowledged conflicts in their place. These children felt guilty and swore to the world that they would change what it meant to be German, speaking about a responsibility that their parents couldn't or didn't accept.

That is probably the average biographical starting point of today's good people of Germany. Born a generation after the bad people of Germany, they one day asked questions their parents couldn't answer. These young people then discovered that they had to make up for something their parents were incapable of. The good people of Germany wanted to be better than their mothers and fathers, the bad people of Germany.

The good people say that the most barbaric deeds of the century arose from this country. They say that Germans bear a special responsibility when minorities are persecuted; that they in any case bear responsibility for Jews and Gypsies; that all who are persecuted and seek protection have a "right to a place to stay" (which doesn't exist anywhere else). Taste, behavior and vocabulary mark them as people who mistrust anything that is German.

When those belonging to the line of people victimized by Germans express these sentiments, they are talking from experience. When Germans who were born or went to school after the war speak in this way, they are not only distancing themselves from the nationalist tone but are also, suspiciously, declaring themselves free and clear of the local tradition of nationalism. Those who speak that way are far more entangled than they believe in the nationalism from which they distance themselves. They are *negative nationalists*, using the vocabulary of nationalism and yet turning the meanings around. They respond to the decisions and slogans of current right-wing extremists with a reversal of positions. The call for a right to a place to stay simply reverses the simple slogan "Foreigners get out of here!"

In the Germany of the 90s there is an alarming rise in incidents of xenophobia and persecution. Meanwhile, the other side cultivates its xenophilia and positive racism. If right wingers say, "Germany for the Germans," the ones who turn things around say, "Never again Germany."

Every good person of Germany, negative nationalist or positive racist, had to hate Germany at some point in their life. They suffer because of German history in the way their parents — who would have had reason to suffer — couldn't. Just as the path from caretaker of Jews to murderer of Jews wasn't long, as we learned from Adolf Eichmann's example, so too it's a short path from xenophile to xenophobe. In stipulating that a foreigner is someone special, both attitudes oppose a normalization.

Take, for example, the couple around forty who are trying to decide which school to send their daughter to. The school nearby has a high percentage of foreigners; only German students attend the one further away. The left-wing, liberal parents choose the school further away. To compensate for their decision, since "basically" they "support" a multicultural society, they hire an African cleaning woman.

Nationalism puts one's nation *above* other nations; negative nationalism puts one's nation *below* other nations. Both rely on a notion of inequality, and ideologies of inequality are the basis for every form of extremism. Negative nationalism in Germany is the reaction of the second generation to their parents of the war generation, consciously distancing themselves from older people and unconsciously taking on the attitude they wished their parents had had. These impulses inform the social critics who belong to the second generation. Their negative nationalism, like nationalism, accords special status to Germany. The first generation's lack of responsibility has been followed by the demand on the part of many in the second generation for global responsibility. The negative nationalists acted out of a peculiar power, and now many of those born after them act with a strange powerlessness.

There were reasons to be ashamed of being a German. Often, however, that shame easily becomes an end in itself: my shame in being a German makes me proud, because implicitly I am the better German. Nationalists and their negative counterparts both want to be good Germans, something better than others. As before, identity formation in these parts seems possible only along a special path, whether marked by *pride* or *shame.*

Whoever needs to be seen as an educated person maintains his self-esteem by judging someone else to be stupid. Dieter Hallervorden used to tell a joke about how dear stupidity is to the educated:

A brain-dealer and a client. The dealer offers the brain of a well-known scientist. Its price: 2,500 DM. Later he offers the brain of a Nobel laureate. Its price: 4,000 DM. The prices are per 100 grams, he says, as he pulls down from the shelf the brain of a hooligan. Its price: 40,000 DM. The client asks, "Why is the hooligan's brain so expensive?" The dealer replies,

"Do you have any idea how many hooligans it took to put
together 100 grams?"

Educated people — it's how to recognize their stupidity —
need stupid people.

3.
—

*I*n the 60s, as postwar children forced their survivor-parents into political as well as personal discussions, the first
generation, when hard pressed, pointed to their experiences;
they meant their life experience — the war and the subsequent
austerity (before the time of gluttony). Twenty years later, the second generation, if contradicted, plays up their global education,
claiming they know more about the world beyond Germany. The
younger people of the third generation no longer buy that, any
more than the second generation believed in the first generation's experience.

Just as it was unthinkable for some of the children of the
war parents not to take on responsibility for the welfare of
the Jewish people, it is hard for young people now to imagine
why being proud to be a German should be forbidden —
when, in fact, everyone cheers when German soccer teams
score a goal.

What counts in defining a generation is not the passage of
twenty-five years, but rather the life experience. I see members
of the third generation as those who had teachers of the second
generation and got tired of them; some students reacted to all
the talk about equality by leaning toward ideologies of inequality. The second generation itself was marked by parents who
lived through and survived the war experience and then didn't
talk. These war parents, their children's reaction to them, now
the children's children's reactions — these are the three percep-

tions of reality, the three experiences, that pull the generations apart and at the same time bind them.

Once the country was almost rebuilt, Germans could not manage alone and recruited workers from other countries in order to reach prosperity for all faster. Once again parents and children were sitting down at the table, the grown-up children of the survivor generation having become parents. They wanted to be their children's friends, to be easygoing, to brighten up their everyday life with the fruits of the revolution. They wanted to talk about everything and never force their children to do anything, but always encourage them, at most force them to let themselves be encouraged. And they wanted to question their own authority as educators.

Tellingly, these are exactly the qualities the postwar children missed in their survivor-parents. And now the postwar children's children, who are twenty years old and don't want to deal with history quite yet, have absolutely no understanding for that context. They notice that older people have trouble whenever conversation turns to the land whose citizens we are. That's what they notice when their assertion of pride manages to hack to pieces the others' brooding. The dialogue between the second and third generation is as crude and incomprehensible as the one between the second generation and the first had been. Nowadays it's harder for young people to see through this whole issue because so much time has elapsed between National Socialism and the discussion about it; they can only speak about Hitler and Auschwitz indirectly "in their own interest."

Yet again we get not a conversation but an exchange of prejudices. Some in the third generation, after sitting around the table with their postwar parents, now proclaim they are proud and all the rest. Few sentences so instantly stir up their parents' rage. The pattern of communication is again automatic reflexes, just as it was when the second generation provoked their war parents. The second generation's provocations — "The police are murderers and fascists" — make insinuations about the Third Reich, as do their reflex reactions now to the third generation's provocative "We are proud." The slogans are exaggerations, headlines brought into play when reasonable speech can't get to anyone. Reflex answers slogan, slogan answers reflex. Just as the first generation angrily challenged the second generation to move to the East, so too now many in the second generation call out, "Nazis get out of here!" The second generation doesn't see the parallel, suffering an attack of global responsibility as they sit there with one of the proud ones of the third generation.

Negative nationalists haven't really matured or liberated themselves from daddy, from the father-state. They remain fixated on the state in their infantile line of argument: Father, I have to suffer on your account. Since you never bought me gloves, I have to let my hands freeze!

No generation has been marked with the compulsion to be good like the second has. No other generation has the same fixation on the Third Reich. Having provoked their parents with that topic, they now let themselves be provoked by their children with that same topic.

One author of the second generation offers an interpretation of this fate: a Nazi generation came before him; his generation is enlightened; its offspring are young Nazis. He concludes that the second generation did everything right, except that they should have propagated their antifascist ideas more aggressively. Then there wouldn't be so many problem-cases in the third generation. Absolved! One good generation in between two bad ones.

4.
—

When xenophobia shamelessly displays itself, xenophilia then moves closer to centerstage. Xenophilia is indispensable in the conscience menu of the good people. Xenophiles are conceited imaginary cosmopolitans. They are lots of things, except German, because they never really got over having had to hate Germany. As if in self-defense, they discovered their love for foreign countries, especially for liberation movements on the other side of the earth. Eritrea and Nicaragua became more familiar than Stralsund and Bautzen could ever be.

Those who don't learn from their experience are condemned to repeat it. In the autumn of 1991, inhabitants of Saxon Hoyerswerda drove out the asylum seekers there. For weeks on end, repeated attacks were reported from every part of the republic every evening. Since Hoyerswerda the new right-wing extremism has become inescapable; TV shows were made and movements were started to oppose the open racism. Every talk show had to take up the topic at least once. Moderators and producers tacitly agreed that it was high time to speak, not *with* right wingers, but *about* them. One of the few exceptions was the women's TV magazine "Mona Lisa," which invited a female politician from the National Party to say what she thought and others who contradicted her. It could have been routine; it was an exception.

A special report broadcast live on ARD from the town square in Hoyerswerda got out of control. To provide authentic backdrop, skinheads of the extreme right were permitted in the back rows. Inevitably, they sometimes took over the show with their singing. Moderators were ashamed by what they had produced and immediately expressed their outrage and made excuses; producers compulsively came up with ideas for doing something against the right wing and every three days invited notable non-Germans, well-known from TV, to their studios to confirm for the *n*th time that we are not a xenophobic country. It should be reassuring when the African American comedian Ron Williams says that, personally, he has never had problems as a foreigner in Germany.

A year later, framed by a shameless asylum debate and an ever more emphatic xenophilia, inhabitants of Rostock-Lichtenhagen drove out the asylum seekers there. Once again attacks occurred every night for three months. The Germans had to go through this experience twice because they didn't learn the first time. In the eleven months between Hoyerswerda and Rostock, both xenophobia and xenophilia seemed simply to intensify. Two senseless coalitions are intent on proving they're right in front of the other, failing to notice that they are merrily digging democracy's grave. It seems as if the country consists only of pyromaniacs — some start fires, others hold candles. Ron Williams now reports that he has been harassed in Munich.

Munich, Hamburg and Essen shone in the glow of chains of candles. Frankfurt and Berlin rocked against the right. Opel and Tengelmann called for tolerance in oversize ads. One Saturday afternoon federal division soccer players wore shirts with the logo *My friend is a foreigner*. There was music against xenophobia and dance against racism. The Social Democratic Party called for *Tolerance — to avoid even further damage*. The tips of the day were *Buy your fruit in the Turkish store, Next time on the subway, take a seat next to an African*. I heard *Without foreigners we'd be alone* and read *Everyone is a foreigner*. I read *Germany, shut up! — Foreigners, please don't leave us alone with these Germans — Foreigners come in, Rheinlanders get out of here! (Ausländer rein, Rheinlander raus)*. And *At least one less Germany*. A newspaper had a campaign with the title

Foreigners, come here, and called for a foreign percentage of twenty to thirty percent "in order to stop the mob, which is hard to rein in, from beating up a small minority."

With a few exceptions these kinds of captions and slogans did not emerge after Rostock, as one might think, but the year before, after Hoyerswerda. Xenophilia spread out to all corners of the republic in the autumn of 1991. The intention of all these campaigns and slogans is to do something against current right-wing extremism. Realizing that Rostock and the waves of attacks came after all this, we might conclude what we might have guessed earlier: that all those campaigns only serve to improve the self-image of their promoters. The bad German person wasn't about to let a good talking-to stop him from being bad.

For a few weeks people talked about a poster containing the names of prominent Germans under the heading *I am a foreigner.* Those responsible for it told me the point was to sell xenophilia like a product — laundry detergent, perhaps. Everyone knew that none of the individuals listed was a foreigner, just as everyone knows the difference between tourists loaded with traveler's checks and political refugees. The poster meant to draw attention to itself by ignoring those differences. Hans Magnus Enzensberger calls such advertising "untruthful," as if there were any other kind.

Right after Hoyerswerda, the organizer of a rock concert found himself faced with a hundred and twenty bands who wanted to play at Rock Against the Right in the Deutschlandhalle in Berlin, but only twelve got to perform because of time constraints. Since then, a hundred and eight bands consider the organizer their enemy. On top of it, Turkish youths accused him of xenophobia because they weren't granted free admission to the anti-racism concert. He said he'd never do anything like that again and wasn't heard from after Rostock.

The opponents of the right wingers are not united. Some just want to beat up the stone-throwers, and others want discussions to prevent anyone from applauding when the stone-throwers act. Although both are against the right, they end up seeing each other as enemies, the one accused of underestimating the danger, the other of overdoing it.

Every reaction seems false, in keeping with the lethargy of recent years, during which the new right-wing extremism developed and moved to the center, while everyone was paying no attention and pursuing their 80s fun. Now they act as if there just hasn't been time to think about what to do. It is true that if you don't think about what you're doing, you'll do the wrong thing. The initial reaction, emphatic xenophilia, needs to be followed by other responses that do justice to both sides. Instead, everyone has stayed at the infantile level of spitefulness — "Now I'll show you" — and the so-called asylum debate, the radicalization on the streets and the multicultural appeasements have gone on for years with no end in sight.

In the first decades after the war young Germans had to come to terms with old Nazis, and they managed. Now we have to come to terms with that generation's own preoccupation with the Third Reich. The xenophiles make me smile just as much as the prophets of doom they were ten years earlier or the revolutionaries against the system they were twenty years ago. They've done it all only for daddy — who wouldn't talk to them — and have meanwhile risen through the ranks of the institutions. Germany, once full of disabled war veterans, now is full of disabled postwar veterans.

5.

My phone started ringing more frequently after the week of fires in Rostock-Lichtenhagen. I was invited to lectures and discussions, whether in Karlsruhe, Bremen,

Cologne, Aachen or the Bavarian Forest, in Berlin-Mitte, Constance, Hamburg or Frankfurt: everywhere people were telling themselves that *in this area* there are a mere handful of right-wing extremists, we know who they are and have them under control. This notorious remark corresponds in any case to the notoriety the smallest places in the republic achieve after right-wing extremists have left their mark there. I'd heard the reassuring formula when I was in Constance and the next morning read that graves had been vandalized on the other side of the lake in Überlingen.

Why were the grownups who discussed all this so boring, the students so interesting? Only in schools was there the beginnings of the social discussion this topic deserves; only there did some dare not to posture as better persons. Instead, they made calls for tougher punishment or full-time employment for Nazis or criticized those proposals, and in the end were honest enough to say that they didn't give a shit about the whole thing, that they were in school to work on their careers, period. The grownups, on the other hand, apparently came with the goal of promoting their good intentions and sharing their humanitarianism. Quickly everything got watered down, and the conversations lost their edge from so much goodness. The grownups merely reassure each other until the next morning's newspaper arrives to shock them again.

And then there are the conflicts in their humanitarianism! They support tough law enforcement, the full force of the law, as they say, but they are scared stiff at the thought of demanding fuller prisons. They always opposed the security measures of Paragraph 129 but now want them used against right-wing extremists. They demand the absurd right for everyone to stay, but in their government positions pass resolutions that achieve the opposite.

I am therefore grateful to those who, without intending it, have brought to light the taboos of the enlightened who gather at such discussions: like the woman from a wealthy left-liberal household who didn't dare tell her husband that an asylum seeker had stolen her purse after she, out of pure humanitarianism, sat herself down in the middle of a group of asylum seekers, acting the good German; or the woman who works in a home for asylum seekers and said in public that every day she's afraid of going to work and that one of her female colleagues had been mistreated. These two women provoked reactions that had not been agreed upon in advance.

Bad young person, come on, be good, murmur the good people, which of course angers the young people. The solution becomes the problem. The good person is divided and busily weighs the good against the bad, while the bad person, with the undeniable advantage of not being divided, has nothing to weigh. He is bad.

6.

On a stage, the special position of a king doesn't become manifest from his behavior alone; it takes subjects who behave like subjects to make a king of the man in costume. So, too, good people are nothing without bad people. Only the latter can bring the former into relief. That's half the dilemma: good people are reactive characters who live off the bad people. If they don't conjure up someone, they have nothing to say: Big Brother, Star Wars, Ronald Reagan (who for his part coined "the Evil Empire"), Helmut Kohl, German unification. The good people assign themselves the role of admonishing and warning, of being experts on the long-term effects of current political decisions. It's hard to pin down what they're really arguing, since they claim to think beyond "the particular moment" or "the current situation." By thinking "in terms of society as a whole" or "globally," they display their obvious education and by implication their intellectual superiority. The other half of the dilemma is that the bad people then get really angry when the good people try to show them what they are doing wrong. The bad person realizes, if he hadn't already, exactly where he stands as soon as stupid assumptions, stigmatization and prejudice come up.

Negative nationalism has long been a part of everyday life, but now the escapism it entails is becoming clear. The theme always seemed a bit exaggerated, too emphatic, but since 1990 the issue is the present rather than projected fears about the future. The one argument I heard against German unity was that a big Germany would be dangerous. Leading negative nationalists won't let go of that position. Every problem caused by the unification process proves them right, so they don't participate in the debate about how this inevitably large country should look and function in the future, how it should be governed. They leave the pragmatic answers to those they grouchily turn their backs on. What is this if not spitefulness? If there is a problem, they are the first to complain, but their critique has turned into whining. Nationalists and negative nationalists are the least likely to be bothered by a changing reality.

Negative nationalism is increasing the risks, because the question at issue is not a social game or a novel, but whether or not we still desire and understand the need for a democracy. In their rhetoric the negative nationalists, as much as their political opponents, obscure the important concerns.

It's becoming ever clearer that the notorious phrase *Germany? No thank you* is as destructive as a nationalist attitude, because this escapism does not confront the real question behind all the superficial ones: will this country, large and no longer under occupation, take its rightful position in the international arena or won't it? Without megalomania *and* without compulsive self-denigration. Can we call migration movements migration movements, or do we choose a term like parasite, which refers to our fear instead of the factual situation? Can we call youth-in-revolt youth-in-revolt, or are we so weak that we have to conjure up "Neo-Nazis"?

The danger posed by negative nationalists and conceited imaginary cosmopolitans is that their pure oppositionality can ruin the search for a compromise. They run the risk of not recognizing the pertinence of nationalist contents and, by the very fact of not taking it seriously, indirectly promoting it.

There are plenty of crazy people ready to butt heads with each other, but we now need to find positions that get out of the paradoxical intergenerational communication; we need to start talking about real matters and stop using alibi topics like *foreigners yes* or *foreigners no*. Why follow either those who spout, "Finally we are somebody again!" or those who fret that megalomania and chauvinism are taking over? How can I express what I'm for and against without becoming a pyromaniac starting fires or lighting candles? The civil, livable position has yet to be found.

7.
—

I meet people who don't want to be reminded of the war. I meet people who say the war created a moral obligation on the part of those born later. And I meet people for whom the war has no relevance and who, lacking inhibitions, insist on overturning inhibitions. All these attitudes are understandable, for they all derive from history, an undeniable history that everyone is reacting to. What else can be expected? The normal and best case imaginable would be for these three generations to communicate their attitudes to one another. Instead, again and again communication gets displaced by ideological finger wrestling.

What's missing is empathy for people regardless of their ideology. The second generation's usual reaction is politically moribund. First it regurgitates the Left-Right scheme and then loads up its arguments with references to the Third Reich and the Third World. First classification, then condemnation. When even the "simplest minds" don't go for it, the second generation's superior intellectuals retreat to discussing individual cases.

But this intelligentsia can offer no intelligent proposals on how to talk to those who assert their pride in being German. Rather, they play up their own intellectual superiority to indict those who lack education. Many of our enlightened people believe they are the only enlightened people and would never grant that status to anyone who feels burdened by foreigners.

8.

Walter Jens, standing at the podium of the Academy of Arts in Berlin, has two examples to tell. Youth watch breakfast TV without breakfast and afterwards beat each other up. It's just as bad, he thinks, that the people who point to this are insulted for being "good people." For him the very fact that "good person" could become a term of abuse is a sign of the "brutalization of humankind."

I am not in the habit of insulting "good people." The point, rather, is to call attention to a fate; the second generation was destined to be marked by parents who wouldn't talk and therefore couldn't be believed when they did. The private impulses that led to "1968" came out of that experience. Just as the first generation was destined to participate in the war, the second generation was destined to develop its own frame of reference in the postwar period. It was forced to provoke a generational revolt and the defend its position vis-à-vis those born later. The fate of the good people is becoming more visible as their arguments prove anachronistic in a society that is leaving the "1968 and after" period. Only now have the limitations in their thinking shown through, and they themselves are now revealed to be living in their own past. It's not unkind to say they have the fate of the *good person*, for they too do evil, but always for good reasons.   ⱽ

Translated by Andrés J. Nader

CONTRIBUTORS

Ida Fink was born in Poland and lives in Israel. She is the author of *The Journey*, a novel, and *A Scrap of Time*, a collection of stories which received the Anne Frank Prize for Literature. In 1995 she was awarded the Yad Vashem Prize, a tribute for writing about the Holocaust. "The Baker's Ongoing Resurrection" is from her newest collection of stories, *Traces*, published by Metropolitan Books, Henry Holt and Company.

Han Ong, 29, is a high school dropout and recent recipient of a MacArthur Fellowship. Born in the Philippines, he came to the United States in 1984. His plays have been performed in the U.S. and England. He is preparing to direct a film based on his first screenplay, *Cantonese Pop Star*.

Rose Moss was born in South Africa and has lived in Boston since 1964. She is the author of two novels, *The Family Reunion* and *The Terrorist* (published in South Africa as *The Schoolmaster*) and a nonfiction account of a political trial, *Shooting at the Crocodile*. She has been shortlisted for a National Book Award and is a fellow of MacDowell and Yaddo, and now teaches at Harvard.

Francesc Torres is a multimedia artist, videomaker and writer. Born in Barcelona, he moved to the United States in 1972 and lives in New York City. Solo exhibitions include the Whitney Museum of American Art, the Carnegie Institute Museum, the Hirshhorn Museum and the Museo Nacional Centro de Arte Reina Sofía, Madrid. His awards include several NEA Fellowships and the DAAD Fellowship, Berlin. He has written extensively on art, culture and politics and contributes regularly to *El País*.

Scott L. Malcomson is a frequent contributor to the *New Yorker*. He is the author of *Empire's Edge: Travels in Southeastern Europe, Turkey and Central Asia* and the forthcoming *One Drop of Blood: A Personal History of Racial Separatism*.

Leo Ou-fan Lee is the author of *The Romantic Generation of Modern Chinese Writers* and *Voices from the Iron House: A Study of Lu Xun*. He writes frequently for journals in Hong Kong, Beijing and Taiwan. His cultural column, "Ravings from the Fox's Den," appears in Chinese in the *Hong Kong Economic News*.

John Brenkman is the author of *Culture and Domination* and *Straight Male Modern: A Cultural Critique of Psychoanalysis.*

Anne McClintock is the author of *Imperial Leather: Race, Gender and Sexuality in the Colonial Contest.* She has edited, with Aamir Mufti and Ella Shohat, *Dangerous Liasons: Gender, Nation, and Postcolonial Perspectives.* She also edited a special issue of *Social Text,* "Sex Workers and Sex Work." She is currently completing *Skin Hunger: A Chronicle of the Sex Trade* and editing a collection entitled *Screwing the System.*

Wayne Koestenbaum's most recent book is *Jackie under my Skin;* his other works of criticism are *Double Talk: The Erotics of Male Literary Collaboration* and *The Queen's Throat: Opera, Homosexuality, and the Mystery of Desire.* His volumes of poetry are *Ode to Anna Moffo and Other Poems* and *Rhapsodies of a Repeat Offender.*

Hugo Achugar, who lives in Montevideo, won Uruguay's national poetry prize for *Orfeo en el salón de la memoria* in 1991; two other recent books of poems are *Las mariposas tropicales* and *El cuerpo del Bautista.* As a critic, he has published several books, including most recently *La balsa de Medusa* and *La biblioteca en ruinas,* which won two national prizes for criticism. He also wrote the novella *Cañas de la India* under the pseudonym Juana Caballero.

Bodo Morshäuser, a journalist and fiction writer, lives in Berlin. He has won several prizes for his fiction. His short story collections are *Die Berliner Simulation* and *Blende;* he is also the author of *Nervöse Leser, Hauptsache Deutsch* and *Warten auf den Führer.* "The Good Persons of Germany" is the first of his work to appear in English.

GENEROUS SUPPORT FOR THE EDITORIAL AND
ARTISTIC PREPARATION OF **VENUE** IS PROVIDED BY

THE SCHOOL OF LIBERAL ARTS AND SCIENCES,
BERNARD M. BARUCH COLLEGE,
CITY UNIVERSITY OF NEW YORK.
ALEXANDRA W. LOGUE, DEAN.
LOIS S. CRONHOLM, PROVOST.
MATTHEW GOLDSTEIN, PRESIDENT.

WORLD WIDE WEB ADDRESSES
Additional information is also available through the Publisher's web home page site at http://www.gbhap.com. Full text on-line access and electronic author submissions may also be available.

ORDERING INFORMATION
Four issues per volume. 1997-98 Volume: 1.

Orders may be placed with your usual supplier or at one of the addresses shown below. Claims for nonreceipt of issues will be honored if made within three months of publication of the issue. See Publication Schedule Information. Subscriptions are available for microfilm editions; details will be furnished upon request. All issues are dispatched by airmail throughout the world.

SUBSCRIPTION RATES BASE list subscription price (four issues): US $38.00, GB £26.00, ECU 32.00.* This price is available only to individuals whose library subscribes to the journal OR who warrant that the journal is for their own use and provide a home address for mailing. Orders may be sent directly to the Publisher and payment must be made by personal check or credit card.

Separate rates apply to academic and corporate/government institutions. Postage and handling charges are extra.

*ECU (European Currency Unit) is the worldwide base list currency rate; payment can be made by draft drawn on ECU currency at the current conversion rate set by the Publisher. Subscribers should contact their agents or the Publisher. All prices are subject to change without notice.

PUBLICATION SCHEDULE INFORMATION To ensure your collection is up-to-date, please call the following numbers for information about the latest issue published: 44 (0)118-956-0080 ext. 391; 973-643-7500 ext. 290; or web site: http://www.gbhap.com/reader.htm. Note: If you have a rotary phone, please call our *Customer Service* at the numbers listed below.

For Product Safety Concerns and Information please contact our EU
representative GPSR@taylorandfrancis.com
Taylor & Francis Verlag GmbH, Kaufingerstraße 24, 80331 München, Germany